THE GUNSMITH

392

THE CLINT ADAMS SPECIAL

THE
ALL-ACTION
WESTERN
SERIES

J. R. ROBERTS

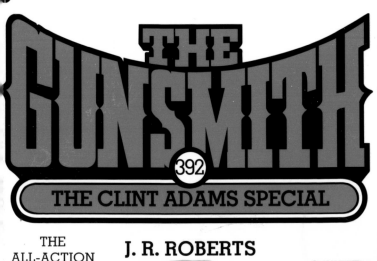

D0030112

RN

TS

$6.99 U.S.
$7.99 CAN

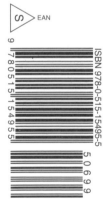

ISBN 978-0-515-15495-5

Staking a Claim . . .

Clint could feel the rifleman's glare burning straight through to the back of his skull. The fellow either believed that he stood outside the range of Clint's pistol or had supreme confidence that he could put Clint down before a shot came his way.

"Where are all those other gunhands you promised?" Clint shouted.

After a few seconds, the man replied, "You'll meet them soon enough, I reckon. That is, unless you want to put an end to this right here and now."

"By handing over the map or by us killing each other?"

"Either one suits me just as well."

Clint moved in closer, to get into pistol range.

"Are you going to tell me who you are?" Clint asked.

"All you need to know is that I'm the man with a rightful claim on this gold."

"If that was the case, you wouldn't need the map."

"Stop splitting hairs, Mr. Adams," the man said in an aggravated tone. "Put an end to this now before things get a whole lot worse."

"You're bluffing. The odds are evened out and you're trying to get what you want through talk."

The man's voice took a steely edge as he replied, "You want more than talk? So be it." He flipped open his coat to reveal the holster strapped to his hip.

NO LONGER PROPERTY
OF ANYTHINK
RANGEVIEW LIBRARY
DISTRICT

DON'T MISS THESE
ALL-ACTION WESTERN SERIES
FROM THE BERKLEY PUBLISHING GROUP

THE GUNSMITH by J. R. Roberts

Clint Adams was a legend among lawmen, outlaws, and ladies. They called him . . . the Gunsmith.

LONGARM by Tabor Evans

The popular long-running series about Deputy U.S. Marshal Custis Long—his life, his loves, his fight for justice.

SLOCUM by Jake Logan

Today's longest-running action Western. John Slocum rides a deadly trail of hot blood and cold steel.

BUSHWHACKERS by B. J. Lanagan

An action-packed series by the creators of Longarm! The rousing adventures of the most brutal gang of cutthroats ever assembled—Quantrill's Raiders.

DIAMONDBACK by Guy Brewer

Dex Yancey is Diamondback, a Southern gentleman turned con man when his brother cheats him out of the family fortune. Ladies love him. Gamblers hate him. But nobody pulls one over on Dex . . .

WILDGUN by Jack Hanson

The blazing adventures of mountain man Will Barlow—from the creators of Longarm!

TEXAS TRACKER by Tom Calhoun

J.T. Law: the most relentless—and dangerous—manhunter in all Texas. Where sheriffs and posses fail, he's the best man to bring in the most vicious outlaws—for a price.

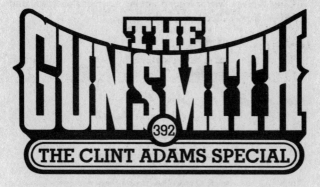

THE GUNSMITH

392

THE CLINT ADAMS SPECIAL

J. R. ROBERTS

JOVE BOOKS, NEW YORK

THE BERKLEY PUBLISHING GROUP
Published by the Penguin Group
Penguin Group (USA) LLC
375 Hudson Street, New York, New York 10014

USA • Canada • UK • Ireland • Australia • New Zealand • India • South Africa • China

penguin.com

A Penguin Random House Company

THE CLINT ADAMS SPECIAL

A Jove Book / published by arrangement with the author

Copyright © 2014 by Robert J. Randisi.
Penguin supports copyright. Copyright fuels creativity, encourages diverse voices,
promotes free speech, and creates a vibrant culture. Thank you for buying an authorized
edition of this book and for complying with copyright laws by not reproducing, scanning,
or distributing any part of it in any form without permission. You are supporting writers
and allowing Penguin to continue to publish books for every reader.

JOVE® is a registered trademark of Penguin Group (USA) LLC.
The "J" design is a trademark of Penguin Group (USA) LLC.

For information, address: The Berkley Publishing Group,
a division of Penguin Group (USA) LLC,
375 Hudson Street, New York, New York 10014.

ISBN: 978-0-515-15495-5

PUBLISHING HISTORY
Jove mass-market edition / August 2014

PRINTED IN THE UNITED STATES OF AMERICA

10 9 8 7 6 5 4 3 2 1

Cover illustration by Sergio Giovine.

This is a work of fiction. Names, characters, places, and incidents either are the product
of the author's imagination or are used fictitiously, and any resemblance to actual persons,
living or dead, business establishments, events, or locales is entirely coincidental.

If you purchased this book without a cover, you should be aware that this book is
stolen property. It was reported as "unsold and destroyed" to the publisher, and neither
the author nor the publisher has received any payment for this "stripped book."

ONE

"We're rich! We're goddamned, god-blessed, filthy, stinkin' *rich!*"

Clint stood at the mouth of a cave that was stuck deep in a desert south of the Texas border. Apart from a bunch of lizards and scorpions, it seemed that nobody had set foot there in years . . . perhaps decades. The man beside him, however, had been a bit more optimistic. Despite all the evidence to the contrary, he swore up and down that other men had been to that cave. Not only that, but those same men had left something behind. Until this moment, Clint had been satisfied to let him dream. Now he started to believe there could be more to it than that.

George Oswalt was hunched over in a dark corner of the cave. Because of his wild mane of hair, thick build, and heavy breathing, he seemed more like a creature that would live in such a place. When he'd stood up to hold his arms up high and waved them over his head to make himself even taller than his normal six feet three inches, he looked even more like a bear.

"You see this?" George hollered. In one hand was a dusty pouch and in the other was something that glittered in the faint bit of light from the lantern Clint was carrying. "See this here? I was right! I was right!"

"Take a breath, George," Clint said. "I'm still trying to figure out how we could be both god-blessed and goddamned."

George's round face twisted into a confused expression beneath a mask of coarse, dark brown whiskers. "Huh? Oh. What?"

"Never mind," Clint said. "Let me get a look at what you've got there."

More than happy to share his find, George hurried forward so quickly that he almost stumbled over the uneven surface of the cave's floor. He stretched out both hands while sputtering, "This is it! It's here! It's really here! I can't believe it. I mean . . . I do believe it, but . . . I can't . . ."

"George?"

"Yeah?"

"Shut up."

George was about to say something to that, but opted to nod instead.

Clint held the lantern up a bit so more of its light could shine down onto George's hands. His attention was first caught by the left hand, which held several dirty coins. He took one of the coins from George and held it right next to the lantern for a closer look.

"Well?" George asked in an excited whisper. "Is that what I think it is?"

The coin was rough around the edges and stamped with a simple design. Obviously, it had been melted down and cast by someone other than the United States Treasury. Even so, that wouldn't have much impact on its value if it passed the rest of the tests. For now, however, Clint could only go with what he had, which were his senses and experience.

He rubbed the coin between his finger and thumb. He tossed it a few inches into the air so he could feel its weight when it came down to slap against his palm. Finally, he clamped it between his teeth so he could look for indentations.

"Far as I can tell," Clint admitted, "it's gold."

George clenched his fist around the rest of the coins in his hand so he could pump that hand into the air as he shouted, "*Hot damn!*"

"Let's see the rest of them."

George handed them over along with the pouch he'd been carrying so he could return to the corner where his celebration had begun. "I knew it! I knew there'd be something here, I just knew it!"

Now that he had more than one coin in his hand, Clint got a better feel for their weight and texture. He'd held plenty of gold in his day, and he was certain he was doing so again. "Yeah," he said. "You knew it, all right. Even so, let's take this back to town so we can be absolutely certain."

"You are certain! You just said so yourself!"

Knowing it wouldn't do much good to argue while George was so worked up, Clint opened the pouch and took a look inside. There were only three or four more coins in there, and they looked just like the ones in his hand. He dumped the coins he was holding back into the pouch, folded the top over, and tucked it into his pocket. "Let's see what else you found," he said while walking over to join George in his corner.

George's enthusiasm was just as explosive when he turned his attention back to his discovery. "Look here, Clint! I found this underneath a shelf of rock. Come see."

The cave itself was wide but stretched back less than ten yards. While the mouth of the opening was large enough for a horse to enter, the ceiling sloped downward at a steep enough angle to force the men to stoop over before they got all the way to the back. George hunkered over about halfway inside the cave where the shadows got thick enough to require the use of the lantern. This was one of nearly a dozen caves they'd explored that day. In the days before that, they'd poked around into so many holes and caverns that Clint had lost count of them.

On the ground directly beside George's feet was a pile of flat rocks that were all big enough to use as dinner plates. The wall of the cave formed an alcove with a top edge that protruded from the vertical surface in a peculiar way. Extending his arm to shed some more of the lantern's light into the alcove, Clint said, "There's tool markings and jagged edges in there. That was definitely hollowed out by a pickax."

"Or possibly blasted out with dynamite," George offered.

"Could be. It's certainly not natural, though."

"Of course it ain't. Jeb Preston would've made little hidey-holes like this one before he was killed to make certain his money stayed safe."

Clint laughed. "There's no way to know this is Preston's money."

"You think we just happened to stumble upon someone else's gold in these caves?" George's eyes were wide as he looked up and around as though he fully expected to find more valuables protruding from the stone walls around him. "This is Preston's money and this is only the start of it."

TWO

Trujillo was only eight miles from the cave where George had made his discovery, but the town felt like it was about a thousand miles away from the rest of the civilized world. There were only two streets worth mentioning, bisected by a third. Any other path was either an alley cutting between dusty buildings or ruts in the ground that led to nowhere in particular. Since there were no signs on either of the two larger streets, Clint named them First and Second. The one cutting across them was named Cruces, and it was at the northwest corner of First and Cruces that Clint found himself later that day.

Now that the sun had begun its descent, the wind blowing in from the desert had lost some of its scalding touch. Clint stood inside a small shop owned by a horse trader named Ramon. Apart from horses, Ramon also dealt in gold. He was a short fellow who seemed even smaller due to a back that had been bent to an uncomfortable angle after years of hunching over one river or another in search of his next fortune. His scalp, bare except for a few wayward strands of black hair plastered down with spit and sweat, had the same coarse texture as the desert floor. When he scratched it, the dry scraping sound rolled through the stagnant air within his place of business.

"Well?" George asked expectantly. "You satisfied?"

Ramon looked down at the flat stone on the counter in front of him, placed the stopper back into the small vial of acid he'd been using, and gave his head one last scratch. "It's gold," he declared.

"I told you!"

Where George nearly jumped up and down with enthusiasm, Clint kept his arms stoically crossed and his eyes gazing calmly through the dirty glass of the window in front of him. "What about the markings on the coins?" he asked. "Have you ever seen the like?"

"*Sí.*"

"Where?"

Ramon picked up the coin he'd been testing and grazed the tip of his thumb over its surface. The calluses on his hands were so thick that he didn't even feel the sting of the acid that remained in the grooves etched into the gold. "*El General.*"

George squinted at the bald man behind the counter. "*El henner* . . . what now?"

"*El General,*" Clint said, pronouncing each word just as well as someone who'd been born south of the border. "He was some sort of Army officer?"

"I think so," Ramon said. "He just wants us to call him that."

George stepped forward. If there'd been a chair for him to use, he would have perched on the edge of it. "What's his real name?" he asked.

Looking at both other men in turn, Ramon said, "*Señor* Preston."

Slapping the countertop so hard that he nearly spilled the vial of acid, George spun around on the balls of his feet. "Told you! Hot damn!"

Ramon didn't share the other man's enthusiasm. He simply put his acid away before it ruined his counter, and then he stored the flat stone out of sight. "You want to sell these coins?" he asked.

"Yer damn right I do!"

Before the haggling over price could begin, Clint said, "I'm getting something to drink down the street."

"I'll be along shortly," George replied without taking his eyes off Ramon.

Clint stepped outside, more than happy to let the other two men squabble over percentages and pennies. He walked to the corner and headed straight down Cruces Street to a wide building situated almost exactly between First and Second. The saloon was called Tres Burros. Judging by the way the three crudely drawn animals on the sign were butting heads, however, it seemed that whoever had painted the sign didn't know the difference between a donkey and a ram. Fortunately, Clint didn't frequent the place to admire its artwork.

As Clint approached the bar, the man behind it looked his way and said, "There you are, Mr. Adams. Can I set you up with a beer?"

"Do you have to ask, Danny?"

"I suppose not."

By the time Clint picked his spot at the bar and placed one foot upon the tarnished brass rail next to a spittoon, a mug of frothy brew was waiting for him. He picked it up, brought it to his mouth, and tipped it back. The dark, potent beer did a fine job of washing away the dust that he'd brought back with him from the surrounding desert.

"That," he sighed gratefully, "is just what the doctor ordered."

The bartender frowned.

"What doctor?" Danny asked.

Clint shook his head.

"Never mind."

THREE

Tres Burros was one of the larger places in town. Of course, since most buildings in Trujillo didn't even have a second floor, that wasn't saying much. The bar ran along one side of the main room, and a small stage was on the other. In between, there were several round tables and a rectangular one used for faro. Counting the dealer and the single player trying to buck the tiger, there were only eight other people in the saloon at the moment. Since none of them required a refill of their drinks, Danny stayed close to Clint and busied himself with cleaning shot glasses.

"So," Danny said after a few more seconds. "Where's Mr. Oswalt?"

"George should be along soon."

"Is he at Ramon's shop?"

Clint looked up from his mug and asked, "Why do you ask that?"

"Because you two found something in one of them caves, didn't you? Isn't that what he was hooting and hollering about when you two rode into town?"

Actually, Clint wouldn't have been surprised if the

entire town had heard George carrying on when they were still at the cave. "We did find a little something."

"Gold?"

"Not sure. That's why we went to see Ramon."

Even though Clint had tried to keep an even tone and a vaguely bored expression, Danny looked at him as if a mountain of riches had been uncovered less than a mile outside of town. "How much gold did you find?"

Clint could see a few of the other men in the saloon turning to look at him and could feel several more sets of eyes searing into his back. "Not a lot," he replied. "And like I already mentioned, we don't know if it's gold."

As he'd been talking, the narrow door near the end of the bar was opened and a woman dressed in a simple brown skirt and loose-fitting white blouse emerged from a back room. "I thought I heard your voice, Clint," she said. "Come back here, will you?"

Although some of the other customers inside the place were looking toward the bar again, they were most definitely not taking much notice of Clint. The woman standing in the doorway to the back room had full curves that could not be hidden by the loose-fitting clothing she wore. Her hips were wide and round. Her breasts swayed with every motion, and her long, dark hair flowed over her shoulders. She acknowledged all the hungry stares from the customers with a little smile and an upward nod to a few of them. When Clint stepped past her into the back room, she turned away from the others and shut the door behind her.

"So?" she asked anxiously. "Was George full of hot air like always?"

"Not quite."

Her features brightened into a wide smile. "So there was something in those caves?"

"Just one cave, but . . . yes."

"Gold?"

Clint let the question hang in the air for a few moments before he stepped up close to her and whispered, "Yeah. It's gold."

She straightened up and pressed both hands against her mouth so she could muffle the scream that was bubbling just beneath her surface. Any moment, it seemed she would lose control and let the whole town know just how excited she was. Instead of hollering out loud, she reached out to grab Clint's face in both hands and press her lips against his mouth.

Clint was somewhat surprised by her sudden move, but recovered quickly enough. His hands soon came to rest on her hips, and he returned her attentions with ample enthusiasm. And almost as quickly as she'd started the kiss, she broke it off.

"Was it Preston's gold?" she asked.

"The whole Preston story is just that, Drina. It's a tall tale."

"There was a man named Preston who lived around here, Clint!"

"I know. I even did some work for a Preston who lived in this county some time ago. Preston isn't exactly an uncommon name."

Drina's eyes sparkled with unbridled excitement. "There should have been markings. A brand or something . . ."

"There were, but . . ."

"There were? Did anyone recognize the markings?" Drina asked in a rush.

As much as Clint wanted to say otherwise, he told her, "Yes. There were markings on the gold."

"And?"

"And . . . George said he thought the coins we found came from Preston's coffers."

Although Drina was happy to hear that, she restrained herself before asking, "Did anyone else tell you anything?"

Clint sighed, knowing there was no way he could get out of this without stirring her up even more. Even if he tried to float a lie past her, it would only be a matter of time before George came along with a conflicting story. "Ramon verified that the coins were gold. He also said he recognized the markings."

"Markings from who?"

"El General."

Drina jumped in excitement and then kissed him even harder than before. Within seconds, her hands had wandered down the front of his body to start eagerly tugging at his belt buckle.

"What are you doing?" he asked, although her intentions were becoming clearer by the second.

"Celebrating," she said while pulling open his shirt.

Grabbing on to her ample hips, Clint decided to indulge her. Perhaps stirring Drina up had some advantages, after all.

FOUR

Once they both gave in to the urges that raced through their bodies, Clint and Drina didn't have to say a word. Their hands raced over each other, pulling at loose clothing and touching whatever bare flesh they could find. Soon, Clint had her skirts gathered up around her waist and was reaching between her legs to feel her damp pussy. When he started rubbing her, Drina leaned her head back and let out a soft moan.

The room was part storeroom and part office. Since the desk looked too old to support her weight, Clint moved Drina toward a row of three barrels lined up against a wall. She shuffled backward until her heels bumped against a barrel. When Clint grabbed her backside, she hopped up and allowed him to set her on top of the sturdy wooden container.

Her eyes were every bit as excited as when she'd been thinking about the prospect of a fortune in gold. When Clint pulled her blouse off and opened her legs wider, she became even more anxious. Drina had already loosened his jeans, so now all she had to do was pull them down past his hips to free his erection. She grabbed his stiff cock in both hands, stroking it until it was even more rigid.

Feeling as if he was about to burst, Clint positioned himself between her legs and guided his penis into her. The barrel was just tall enough to put Drina at the perfect height, and he plunged his rod into her. Drina wrapped her legs around Clint's waist and clasped her hands behind his neck. When he began thrusting in and out of her, she pumped her hips in time to his rhythm.

Soon, the motion of their bodies got the barrel to rocking back and forth. They wouldn't have noticed it if there were no noise involved. The loud thumping of the barrel against the floor, however, was difficult to ignore.

Drina stopped and showed Clint a mischievous smirk. "Did you lock the door?" she asked.

"Didn't think I was supposed to."

She shifted upon the barrel so she could look over Clint's shoulder. The movement was slight, but made it even tougher for him to remain still while inside her.

"We should be quieter," she said. "Not so much knocking against the floor."

"Here," Clint said as he backed up a step and helped her down. Once she was on her feet, he turned her around so her back was to him and then hiked up her skirts again. Leaning close to her ear, he whispered, "Now you just have to try and keep your voice down."

Drina bent over the barrel and widened her stance so she could accommodate Clint's stiff cock. When he entered her from behind, she tossed her hair back and let out a satisfied grunt before quieting herself down again. Clint grabbed her hips in both hands and held her tightly while he pumped in and out of her.

Looking down, Clint was treated to the sight of her wide, rounded hips and generous buttocks. Every time he pounded into her, Drina's entire body trembled. From where he stood, he could bury every inch of his shaft deep inside her. When he pulled her toward him every time he thrust forward, Drina grabbed the barrel and let out a deep, labored breath.

"Yes," she whispered. "Harder."

Clint was more than happy to oblige. He placed one hand upon the small of her back, feeling the contour of her body and the smooth texture of her flesh. With his other hand, he grabbed some of her hair and pulled her head back until her neck was taut. Even from his current angle, Clint could see the wide smile on Drina's face.

Every time he pumped into her, Clint gave her hair a little tug. He could feel her pussy becoming even wetter, which allowed him to slide in and out of her like a piston. When he let go of her hair, Drina turned around to look at him as if to beg him to take hold of it again. Instead, he slapped a hand on the side of her hip and pounded into her.

Before long, they'd built up enough momentum to test her grip on the barrel one more time. Drina gripped it until her knuckles turned white. She then lowered her upper body until her chest was pressed against the top of the barrel. Her back formed an upward slope of taut muscles that shook every time Clint pounded against her. The more Drina fought the urge to make a noise, the more ragged her breathing became. Soon, every exhale sounded more like a growl and she tensed for her approaching orgasm. When it came, she arched her back and clawed at the barrel. Clint could feel her tightening around his rigid member and pushed into her as far as he could go. When he eased out of her, Drina let out a breath that must have emptied her lungs.

She turned and brushed her hair back. "I'm not through celebrating just yet," she said with a hungry smile.

Clint could hear voices in the next room. In fact, he could hear George's voice babbling on in the same excited rush that had been coming out of him ever since they found the caves in the hills outside of town. Clint couldn't make out any exact words, but he didn't have to think very hard to figure out the gist of what George was going on about.

Pushing him against a tall stack of crates, Drina stroked his cock in long, smooth motions. Then she lowered herself to her knees in front of him, opened her mouth, and wrapped her lips around his shaft. When she slid her mouth all the way down to the base of his erection, Clint was no longer concerned with what George was yammering about in the next room. He simply leaned back, ran his fingers through Drina's thick hair, and savored every moment.

She bobbed her head back and forth, sucking him like a stick of candy. Soon her tongue started working as well, sliding against his thick column of flesh. Clint pushed his hips forward out of instinct, and she was eager to devour him further. Drina eventually slid her mouth all the way down, taking him deep into her throat and holding him in place for a long couple of seconds.

"Jesus," Clint exhaled.

The corners of her mouth curled into a smile, and her hands reached up to press against his stomach. As she sucked him faster, she scraped her nails against his skin, moaning softly as he grew even harder in her mouth. Enveloping just the tip of his cock with her lips, she swirled her tongue around him. When she picked up speed again, she seemed to be working for her own pleasure. Drina devoured him greedily and sucked him faster as if she couldn't get enough.

Clint grabbed the back of her head and clenched his eyes shut as he felt his climax swiftly approach. The heat started in his legs and rushed all the way through his entire body. He knew the end would be intense, and when it came, he let out the breath he'd been holding and emptied himself into her.

She drank him down while slowly licking him.

Clint didn't realize his ears had been filled with the rush of his own blood through his veins until his pulse slowed down a bit. When all of his senses returned, he could once again hear the busy sounds of the saloon that was just on the other side of the nearby wall.

Drina eased her head back, and looked up at Clint. "Now that," she said as he helped her to her feet, "is what I call a celebration."

FIVE

Drina stepped out of the back room first, which sent George into an excited frenzy of happy gestures and sputtered exclamations. When Clint emerged from the room a minute or so later, he wasn't even noticed. He had enough time to buy a fresh beer, take a few sips, and then walk over to the spot at the bar where the other two were standing.

"Clint!" George said. "There you are! I was just telling Adrianna here about how successful—"

Stopping him with a firm hand on the shoulder, Clint leaned over to him and said, "Why don't we have our discussion where the whole town can't listen in?"

"Too late for that," Drina said.

George, on the other hand, wasn't about to be swayed from his joyful frame of mind. "Of course, of course," he replied. To the bartender, he added, "And our drinks are on me."

The bartender nodded and lined up three glasses so he was ready when the next round was needed.

Choosing the table at the back of the room in a corner

that faced the front door, Clint put his back to a wall and sat down.

Barely able to contain himself until his backside hit the chair, George asked, "So, Clint, did you have a chance to tell Adrianna about our good fortune?"

"Please don't call me that," she said. "Only my father calls me Adrianna and it sends a cold shiver down my spine."

"We've been going out to those hills for the last few days," Clint explained. "There've been caves in every damn nook and cranny, but we finally found one that had something in it other than bats."

"How did you find it?" Drina asked.

"It was on Preston's map!" George told her in an excited whisper.

"According to what you were told by the man who sold it to you," Clint warned.

"Right, but the markings we found on an old sign outside the cave as well as the ones stamped on them coins," George continued without losing his enthusiasm, "all match the markings on the map that Preston used as his brand."

"Again . . . that's only according to the man who sold us the map."

Drina's eyes bounced back and forth between the two men as they traded off. She was about to say something, but decided against it when George thumped his fist against the table.

"What the hell is your problem, Clint?" George asked. "You think I'm stupid?"

"No. I just think you're mighty eager to believe something. Am I lying when I say we're basically going on the word of that salesman?"

"He wasn't just some salesman."

"Fine," Clint said. "Whatever you want to call him, he

could have scribbled down any markings he wanted onto that map and told you it was the Preston brand."

"He didn't make up the markings, damn it," George snapped. "They were right there on the coins."

Although Clint wanted to point out that the salesman could have seen the coins and copied the marks onto the map, he knew that would only make the conversation loop around a few more times. As it was, he was already feeling dizzy. Fortunately, Drina stepped in to steer them onto a different path.

"Why would anyone want to pass something off as belonging to this Preston fellow anyway?" she asked.

George looked at her as if she'd just inquired as to why there was so much sand in the desert. "Don't you know who the Prestons are?"

"I've heard the name a few times since I got to town," she replied. "But I've only been here less than a year. From what I've heard, the Prestons were just some rich family whose menfolk all held rank in the Army."

"Army men aren't usually the kind who get rich," Clint said.

Happy to have the audience he'd been craving, George leaned forward with his elbows resting on the table and dropped his voice to a hushed, almost reverent, tone.

SIX

"The Preston men weren't rich," George said, "but they served their country. When some of them . . . brothers, I think . . . came home from the War Between the States, they took up as lawmen. Their brand of justice was rougher than most, and when the sheriff of their county was killed, they took over."

"Where was this?" Clint asked.

"Just across the border in Texas," George told him.

"Anywhere near San Antonio?"

After a bit of thought, George said, "I believe so! I must have told this part of the story to you a few times, I reckon."

Clint hadn't heard this part of the story at all, but he simply said, "Go on."

"Well," George continued, "those Prestons kept their town clean, and as more of the family came home to roost, they cleaned up a good portion of their county."

"Until one of them got greedy," Drina said.

Scratching his head, George muttered, "Did I already tell *both* of you this story?"

"No," she said. "I'm just making the leap between overzealous lawmen and someone who comes into the possession of a store of gold."

"It's not far to leap," Clint said. "I take it that greedy fellow was this *El General*?"

George nodded. "Jebediah Preston. Once he came home, he decided the rest of his clan wasn't performing to the best of their abilities. He took it upon himself to hire on some more gunhands, form something close to a small army, and put his kin in charge. Needless to say, Jebediah was at the top of the heap."

"Where does the gold come in?" Clint asked.

Leaning back in his chair, George took a drink before saying, "They brought down a couple outlaw gangs riding through Texas that were probably on their way here to Old Mex. Word has it, between that gang and some other outlaws they wiped off the face of the earth, the Prestons confiscated a pretty healthy sum.

"Usually, whatever money they took was handed in to the town or the county or . . . whatever the hell someone does with money they find that way. But ol' Jebediah didn't see it that way. He figured his men should reap the spoils of war and them that live in his family's care should live better than them who didn't."

"And how did you come to know all this?" Clint asked.

"Lots of folks know," George replied with a shrug. "Some of them that moved on after living in that county spread the word. Some of it leaked out through other means."

"Could have been spread by the Prestons themselves," Drina offered. "Might help scare away any more outlaws thinking to pass too close to the lands under their protection."

Glancing around and leaning forward, George obviously thought he was digging back into the juicier portion of his story. "It wasn't long before them Prestons came into possession of a whole lot of gold. I heard a gang of train robbers ran afoul of them after hitting a locomotive owned by the U.S. Treasury itself. Of course, I also heard one of the Prestons did some exploring even farther south than here and came back with more gold than he could carry. Who knows which is true."

"Or if either of them are," Drina scoffed.

George continued unabated. "What matters is that they got some gold and Jebediah wasn't about to let it go. After years of runnin' his own county as he saw fit, I imagine he lost some of his faculties if you know what I mean." To illustrate his point, George pointed to his temple and grimaced while waggling his finger as if he were tracing the path of a horsefly. "Once he lost his hold on his mind, Jebediah treated his family property like it was his own sovereign country. Minted his own coins and everything."

"That sounds insane," Drina said.

"I already told you Jebediah lost his mind, didn't I?"

"So how would any of that gold wind up in a cave?" Clint asked.

"Maybe some outlaws got lucky, took some from the Prestons, and hid it away," George said. "Maybe Jebediah has more than he can handle and stored it there for safekeeping."

Now Drina was starting to look almost as excited as George. "Maybe they're planning a move into Mexico!" she said in a hurried whisper.

George waggled his eyebrows and said, "It's gotta be something awfully good, but I don't profess to know the details. All I do know is that the man who gave me this map made it known that whoever stashed that gold there won't be coming for it for at least another month. Before Clint asks how I know . . . there's a courier who comes along every

other month and that man I've been talking about found out
that it's gold being carried back and forth across the border.
He sold me the map and will get a cut of the profits. Took
almost every damn penny to my name to get the map, but
I knew it was a good investment. I'll be damned if I weren't
right!"

"All we found was a single pouch," Clint pointed out.
"That's hardly enough to create all this commotion."

Not only did George drop his voice again, but he could
barely be heard by the others at his own table when he
whispered, "That was just one hidey-hole. There's others
in them caves. That way, even if someone stumbles upon
a bit of the gold, they won't find it all."

"We were searching those caves for days," Clint
reminded him. "We were lucky to find what little we did."

"That's because I didn't have much more than a vague
notion of where to start and that's more of a notion than
anyone else ever had. At least, anyone whose last name
ain't Preston. Otherwise, that man who sold the map to me
would've gone after the gold himself." George reached
into his pocket, removed the map, and unfolded it onto the
table. It wasn't much larger than a reward notice for a
wanted man, and he hunched over it to make sure nobody
else in the saloon could get much of a look at it.

SEVEN

It wasn't the first time Clint had seen the map. For that matter, it wasn't even the first map he'd seen that was supposed to lead to some kind of treasure. Some of those maps led somewhere and others didn't. The only consistent profit to be made was for a man who was hired on to help the men who believed the map led somewhere. Clint had hired on as one of those men, which meant he went where he was needed and lent a hand when he could. Until now, George hadn't given him more than a fleeting glimpse of what was on it anyhow.

"These marked caves are in a pattern," George explained. "It's not a straight line, but it's a pattern, and now that we've found one of 'em . . ."

"You just follow the pattern to the others," Drina said.

"That's right."

"If it wasn't getting so close to dark, I'd ride back out there right now," George said as he folded the map and tucked it back into his pocket. "We'll get some sleep and leave at dawn. Ain't that right, Clint?"

"Sure."

George stood up and slapped Clint on the back. "I guarantee you, the rest of this job will be a whole lot easier than what come before. As for you, Adrianna, you won't regret introducing me to Mr. Adams here."

"I did it for a percentage," she said. "Just don't forget to pay up."

"You know I won't." With that, George ambled away from the table and left the saloon.

Turning her attention to Clint, Drina asked, "What's wrong? You don't seem very enthused."

"Something seems familiar about all of this."

"Of course it does. Folks within a hundred miles of the Texas border towns all have some kind of story to tell about the Prestons. Most of it's just that. Stories."

"It's more than just the stories," Clint said. "There's something else." He thought about it while taking a few long pulls from his beer. Tightening his grip on the handle of his mug, he set it down roughly and said, "I just can't put my finger on it."

"You don't have to go along with George. It sounds like all the hard work is done. Maybe I could even—"

"Stop right there," Clint cut in. "You're not going anywhere."

"I can help."

"I'm sure you can, but right now we don't need any more help." Clint drained his beer in one more swallow and set the mug on the table. "You're the one who figured out what George was doing and that I was the man for the job of riding with him, so you've got your ear to the ground. Keep it there and tell me what you find when I get back."

"I still think you're just trying to keep me out of harm's way," she said through a discontented frown.

"You can thank me later."

EIGHT

Dawn came and George was already at the stable when Clint went there to collect Eclipse. The Darley Arabian stallion was always ready for a good run, but George was champing at the bit even more.

"I've been waiting for you!" George said.

"I came here right after breakfast."

"You stopped for breakfast? We could've eaten along the way!"

"A man's got to eat," Clint said. "You'd best have a meal, too. We got a long day ahead of us."

George pulled open the gate of the stall where his own horse was being kept. In one corner of the hay-covered floor was a jacket and bedroll spread out to form what looked like a large nest.

"You never left this stable, did you?" Clint asked.

Looking back to the bedroll, George replied, "I was too worked up to get much sleep, so I stayed here and got everything set for today. I believe I know exactly where to go for the next cave. I did some figuring and—"

Clint stopped him with an upraised hand. "Do you know where we're going?"

"Most definitely."

"Then lead the way. It's too early for the finer details. That is, unless they're something I absolutely need to know."

"Well . . . I suppose you don't need to know."

"Great," Clint said. "You do your job and I'll make sure nobody decides to put a bullet into us."

Clint wasn't necessarily worried about that just then, but his colorful choice of words had their desired effect. George quickly finished his preparations and led his horse outside without any more conversation. Following behind while keeping a severe expression on his face, Clint savored the silence while it lasted. He'd spent more than enough time with George to know it wouldn't last long.

They rode across a few miles of desert terrain without a damn thing moving around them. There was no wind to kick up any dust in front of them. There were no birds circling overhead. There weren't even any lizards scurrying across the trail as far as Clint could see. After another couple of miles, the ground became rocky and the path angled up between some hills. For the better part of the day, one stretch of the trail looked the same as another. Once they got into the hills, however, Clint started to recognize a few landmarks.

"There's the rock formation that looks like a herd of buffalo," George said as he reined his horse to a stop.

Clint pulled back on Eclipse's reins and nodded. "I didn't notice the buffalo part, but I was just thinking how I recall seeing those rocks the last time we were out this way."

"The cave where we found that pouch of gold was just past them buffalo rocks. I'd say around a quarter of a mile. Maybe less."

"Sounds about right."

"I'll need to ride up there and get my bearings," George said. When he saw Clint bow his head and wave him forward, George snapped his reins to get his horse climbing the incline.

Thinking back to what he could remember of the map George had bought, Clint tried to get a rough idea of where to find the next caves that were marked as containing another deposit of Preston's gold. Unfortunately, the map didn't come close to doing justice to what they found. There were caves of all shapes and sized scattered throughout the dusty rocks and tucked behind scorched boulders. The longer Clint looked at them all, the more caves he saw.

"Looks like we've got our work cut out for us," Clint grumbled. Patting the Darley Arabian on the side of his neck, he added, "Don't worry, boy. You won't be expected to walk behind us while we poke our noses into every last one of these damn holes."

Once George was up a ways, he disappeared from sight. Clint didn't think much of it since he fully expected the next couple of days to be spent sniffing around into every hole in that desert. The stash of gold they'd found was a good one, but not nearly as awe inspiring as George insisted it was. If he was right, there was plenty more to be found, but that was only if he was right. Also, there was the matter of finding it all. Whoever had hidden that money wasn't stupid, and they'd done their job well enough for the gold to be safe this long.

Something apart from all of that nagged at the back of Clint's mind. Even worse, he couldn't quite put his finger on what it was. The name "Preston" sounded familiar, and he'd made the connection to that region of Texas, but that was about it. Whatever else there was still drifted just out of reach in the back of his head.

George's boots scraped against the rock on the trail ahead. Pointing Eclipse's nose in that direction, Clint wandered over that way so he was close by if he was needed. Then, he heard an errant step skid on the sandy desert floor to send some loose stones skittering down one of the crooked paths. The only problem was that both sounds had come from distinctly different directions.

"George?" Clint hollered.

It took a few moments, but George poked his head out from a cave that looked to be just large enough to provide him some shade. "Yeah?" he asked.

Now that he knew exactly where George was, Clint shifted his attention toward the other sound he'd heard. There was always the chance that a critter of some kind had upset those rocks. Of course, that would have made things too easy, and Clint knew better than to put much stock in hopes like that.

"Clint? What—"

"Quiet!"

Although George bit his tongue, he emerged from his cave amid the clatter of overanxious feet on uneven ground. In the midst of all of that noise, Clint heard more steps coming from the other direction. They were definitely the steps of a man, and whoever it was, he was doing his best to take advantage of the noise George was making. Clint had already picked up on the noise before, which made finding it again that much easier.

Shifting Eclipse's reins to his left hand, Clint gave them a flick while drawing his modified Colt with his right. The first few seconds after that were the worst. Although he would soon be close enough to get a look at who or whatever was making the noise, his ears were now filled with the rumble of his stallion's hooves against sun-scorched rock.

The first thing he saw was the mouth of the cave where

he and George had discovered that first pouch of gold. The second thing to catch his eye was a man carrying a rifle making his way to a cluster of rocks.

"Hey!" Clint shouted. "Who are—"

He didn't get the rest of his question out before the man swung his rifle around and fired from the hip. The shot was too rushed to hit anything, but came close enough to make Clint nervous. Clint fired a hurried shot of his own just to buy him a second to take proper aim. In that short stretch of time, three more men emerged from the cave George had already plundered.

Unlike the rifleman, the next three didn't make any attempt to sneak or run for the cover of the rock cluster. They simply raised their pistols and opened fire.

NINE

Eclipse had ridden through way too much gunfire to be rattled by the shots that were fired this time, but that didn't mean he intended on staying put to catch one of those bullets. The Darley Arabian turned around and responded quickly to Clint's direction by taking both of them toward the smaller cave George was exploring. Being so familiar with every move the stallion made, Clint could tell Eclipse's footing was uncertain before he was halfway through his turn. He took a quick look down to find sparks flying from the spots where Eclipse's shoes were striking the rock. Rather than slow the horse down, he leapt from the saddle before both of them fell over.

Clint's reasoning may have been sound, but the landing was three kinds of hell. As soon as his feet hit the rocky ground, Clint let out a yelp that told Eclipse to get moving. The Darley Arabian followed the simple command as more gunshots cracked through the air.

"Clint!" George shouted. "You all right?"

"Get back into that cave," Clint hollered.

"I can't!"

"Just go, goddamn it!"

Since the other gunmen had stopped firing, Clint could hear them talking back and forth. The cave from which they'd emerged was just under fifty yards away, so their voices were washed away by the currents of dry air tearing across the Mexican landscape.

Clint had stayed low after dropping from his saddle, and when he rolled onto his side, he could feel every last spot where he'd knocked himself during his landing. He gritted his teeth through the pain and made his way toward the top of the slope so he could get a look at the four men who'd attacked him. The terrain was so uneven that there were any number of places for them to find cover and countless routes for anyone to take if they wanted to get the drop on someone else. Having crawled a short way on his belly, he propped himself up to find two men making their way straight toward him.

Almost immediately, both of those men snapped their eyes toward Clint and took aim with their pistols. Clint rolled sideways as thunder erupted from their barrels. Lead ricocheted against the stone surface where he'd just been, sending sparks into the air and chips of rock spattering against the side of his face.

Stopping himself with an outstretched leg, Clint aimed his Colt as if he were pointing a finger at the closest of the gunmen. He squeezed his trigger once, which was enough to send his target diving for cover. Clint shifted his aim, fired twice, and scrambled to get his feet beneath him.

The next shot that was fired came from the smaller caves behind him. It was the distinctive crack of a rifle, followed by the hiss of a round whipping overhead.

"Come on, Clint!" George shouted. "Run for it!"

Since he wouldn't get a much better opportunity than this one, Clint didn't waste any time in checking the location of the gunmen before accepting George's invitation. Clint kept his head low and moved as quickly as he could toward the caves.

He took less than three steps before pistols were fired at his back. All Clint could do was run faster, and when he was close enough to George's cave, he pushed off with both legs and launched himself head-first toward the shadowy opening.

Once again, Clint's body slapped against the unforgiving desert floor. Both arms were outstretched, so he broke his fall somewhat, which did nothing to ease the discomfort of skidding against the jagged rocks. As soon as the upper portion of his body was in the cooler darkness of the cave, the tips of Clint's fingers smashed against the wall.

TEN

"Damn!" he said while pulling his arms in to recover from his dive. When he tried to sit upright, he cracked his head against yet another uneven surface.

"I told you," George sighed.

Doing his best to at least crouch in the shadows, Clint took a quick inventory of any injuries he'd sustained. So far, there was nothing worse than scrapes, bumps, and bruises. A whole lot of them.

"Told me what?" Clint snapped.

"Told you that I couldn't find much shelter in this cave," George replied. "And before you ask, there's no gold in here either."

A few more shots were fired at them, all of which chipped away at the exterior rock. "Yeah," Clint said. "That's just what I was gonna ask!"

Wincing either from the gunfire or how badly his last few words were received, George asked, "Who are they?"

"Don't know."

"How many are there?"

Clint finished reloading his Colt and snapped the

cylinder shut. "Don't know that either, but I imagine we'll find out real soon."

"How?"

"The hard way."

The rifle in George's hand was the Winchester that had been in the boot of his saddle. Clint knew it was there, but hadn't seen George so much as touch its stock in the time they'd ridden together. Now George held on to it like it was his firstborn.

"How many more rounds do you have for that?" Clint asked.

Before George could answer, Clint snapped his arm out straight in front of his so he could sight along the top of the Colt's barrel. The Colt barked once, filling the little cave with the blast and sending a round toward a gunman who'd been trying to creep up closer to the opening.

"Two," George replied. "Maybe three more shots. I don't know."

"We'll go with two," Clint said as if he was speaking to himself. "If there's any more than that, it'll be a pleasant surprise."

"What do those men want anyway?"

"There's one way to find out." Clint then leaned forward until sunlight touched the front of his face. "Hey! What the hell do you fellows want?"

Clint heard a few of the voices muttering back and forth again before one of them shouted to be heard.

"Found any gold in that cave?" it asked.

Clint put his back to the uneven wall. It was uncomfortable as hell, but at least all of him was concealed when he replied, "Gold? There's a good number of scorpions, but no gold!"

"Scorpions?" George hissed.

Clint silenced him with a harsh glare.

"No gold, eh?" the man shouted. "Then why don't you toss out that map and we can part ways?"

"What about a finder's fee?" Clint asked. He couldn't be less interested in the response to that, but the more he got the other man to talk, the better he could gauge where the attackers were.

"You ain't George," the man shouted. "If you was, I figured we'd already have that map by now. What's your name, mister?"

"Why don't we meet at a saloon back in town and we can introduce ourselves properly?"

As the next few seconds passed in silence, Clint began to entertain the thought that his offer might be accepted. Then things fell back onto the track he'd been expecting.

One shot was fired at Clint and George, which was quickly followed by more. Proving how much could be accomplished when properly motivated, both of them moved all the way to the back of a cave that had less room than an overturned outhouse.

"Maybe we can just wait it out," George said. "They'll run out of ammunition sooner or later."

"Or," Clint replied, "they'll just walk up to the front of the cave and start shooting. Even a ricochet in this hole will likely kill one of us."

"I just don't know who would want to kill me."

"We can figure that out later. Right now, we need to figure out how to live through the next couple of minutes. We got one thing in our favor."

"That's one more than I would have guessed," George whimpered.

Clint inched toward the opening of the cave. As long as he kept quiet, he could hear the sounds from outside even better thanks to the curved rock walls surrounding him. He didn't have far to go before he was outside again, but every fraction of an inch he moved felt like he was running a mile.

Having situated himself with his belly flat against the ground and his eyes fixed on the slope in front of him, Clint waited.

George waited, too, but once his nerves stopped jangling, he got anxious. "What is it, Clint? What's the one thing we got in our favor?"

A minute or so ago, Clint would have knocked George out cold just to keep him quiet. Now, he welcomed a bit of noise. Some of the men outside must have been waiting for that very thing because a subtle rustle announced the fact that one of them was making a move. As soon as he saw a figure cautiously climb the top of the slope, Clint shot it. He'd had all the time he'd needed to steady his aim, so that shot hit its target as best it could from that angle.

The gunman who'd tried to advance was hit in the meat of his neck near the top of his shoulder. Yelping in pain, he straightened up a bit out of reflex, which allowed him to catch Clint's next round squarely through the chest.

"Our advantage," Clint told George, "is that those bastards need to come to us."

"Outstanding!" George said as the first gunman fell over.

"Now comes the hard part."

Shots were already coming from the remaining gunmen to answer for their fallen partner. Every one that cracked through the air caused George to twitch. "Hard part?" he squeaked.

"We can't stay here now, so we gotta charge."

"Ch-Ch-Char—what?"

"It's that or die," Clint said while quickly replacing the rounds he'd spent. "I made my choice, so come with me or stay here."

Instead of waiting for George to find his courage, Clint bolted from the cave.

ELEVEN

As soon as he was out of the cave, Clint took a hard left toward a downward slope that led to an open patch of land about the size of a large corral. The gunmen were through with firing blind. They were taking fewer shots and making them count. Clint dropped to one knee and became still as the rocks. That way, when another of the gunmen approached, he had no trouble hearing him.

The gunman moved up the slope just far enough to see over to the other side where Clint was waiting. Clint waited long enough for the gunman to make himself known. Both men stood their ground for a few seconds until a second gunman stepped up to the other one's side.

"You know it's more than just us two here," the first gunman said to Clint. "There's more of us."

"How did you even know about the map?" Clint asked.

Both gunmen smirked about that one. "Yer partner's got a real big mouth."

"We already brought in the gold," Clint said.

"Then why are you out here?"

The first gunman said, "We know Preston scattered his

gold all over these here hills. You hand over that map, you can keep what you already found and be on your way."

"If I don't?" Clint asked.

"Then you and your friend will be buried in one of these caves."

Clint's pistol was still in his hand, but the other two had theirs ready as well. This wasn't a matter of who was the quicker draw. This was a test of all three's backbone. The one with the steadiest nerves would take a careful shot even while staring down the barrel of another man's gun.

Clint's movements were subtle. All it took was a few muscles to angle his Colt for a proper shot. The instant his gun moved, both of the men in front of him brought their guns up to try and put Clint down.

The second gunman to climb up that slope was the first to pull his trigger. His finger clamped down so hard that the round he fired sailed somewhere off to Clint's right.

Clint took notice of that, but was already committed to shooting gunman number one. He let out part of a breath, squeezed his trigger, and fired a fraction of a second after his target sent a bullet in his direction. Although the gunman missed cleanly, the round from his own modified Colt drilled into the man's chest.

The last gunman in Clint's sight was the one to fire the first panicked shot, and the next one he fired wasn't much better. His round sparked against a rock as Clint's punched through his forehead to explode out the back of his head.

Clint waited for a second as the man in front of him swayed on his feet before dropping heavily to both knees. From there, the man with the bloody third eye crumpled over to join his partner upon the dusty rock.

If there were any gunmen left, they weren't stupid enough to climb up the slope that would bring them in range of Clint's gun. He listened for a hint of movement while replacing the rounds he'd spent with fresh ones from his gun belt.

Instead of waiting for the next shot to be fired, Clint circled around to another narrow path that would take him down the slope in another direction. From what he'd heard from his first shouted conversation, Clint guessed he should be able to get a look at the spot where the attackers had started. After moving carefully around, he climbed up the slope until he could get a look down at the other side.

The man who stood in the distance wasn't trying to hide. He wore a long coat over a blood red shirt tucked into dusty brown pants. There was a rifle in his hands, which he kept in a casual grip in one hand.

Clint could feel the rifleman's glare burning straight through to the back of his skull. The fellow either believed that he stood outside the range of Clint's pistol or had supreme confidence that he could put Clint down before a shot came his way.

"Where are all those other gunhands you promised?" Clint shouted.

After a few seconds, the other man replied, "You'll meet them soon enough, I reckon. That is, unless you want to put an end to this right here and now."

"By handing over the map or by us killing each other?"

"Either one suits me just as well."

Clint moved in closer, to get into pistol range.

"Are you going to tell me who you are?" Clint asked.

"All you need to know is that I'm the man with a rightful claim on this gold."

"If that was the case, you wouldn't need the map."

"Stop splitting hairs, Mr. Adams," the man said in an aggravated tone. "Put an end to this now before things get a whole lot worse."

"You're bluffing. The odds are evened out and you're trying to get what you want through talk."

The man's voice took a steely edge as he replied, "You want more than talk? So be it." He flipped open his coat to reveal the holster strapped to his hip.

The shot to break the silence didn't come from the stranger, and it didn't come from Clint. Instead, it came from another one of the caves, and it sent the unnamed man staggering backward. Rather than crumple from the wound, the man drew his pistol and sent a few quick rounds toward the threat that had just revealed itself. Since he hadn't been expecting to defend himself from that angle, his shots were rushed. The man must have known he didn't stand much of a chance of hitting anything because he finally began to retreat.

"I got him, Clint!" George shouted from his vantage point. There were too many rocks and dry brush along that portion of the slope for Clint to see him, but it was obvious that George had found another cave well away from the first place they'd sought cover.

Clint was careful when he went after the other man. Although he seemed to be running away, there was always the chance that he was simply drawing Clint in close enough for an accomplice or two to pick him off. Someone did hurry toward Clint from one side, but it was his own accomplice in this venture.

"I know I hit him," George said as he rushed to Clint's side. "Looks like he's turning tail."

"Give me that rifle." As soon as he'd holstered his Colt, Clint felt the rifle dropped into his hand. He brought the rifle to his shoulder, sighted along the top of its barrel, but couldn't take his shot before his target disappeared from view. Without taking his eyes from the rocky terrain stretching in front of him, Clint asked, "How many more of them did you find?"

"Only one of them came after me. The rest went to get you."

"And you took care of your man?"

"Yeah," George replied. "More or less. Are we going after that one out there?"

Clint lowered the rifle. "No need. It sounds like he already got to his horse."

As the rumble of hooves against the ground rolled through the air, George said, "Then we should follow him!"

"I doubt it'll do much good."

"Damn it, you're working for me! I say follow him!"

Reluctantly, Clint shrugged. "You're the boss."

TWELVE

Less than an hour later, Clint returned to the expanse of caves dotting the hills. It might have taken him just as much time to find George again if he hadn't spotted a horse's nose protruding from a rock.

Sure enough, the animal was George's, and it was seeking shelter from the oppressive rays of the sun inside a cave with an entrance that was flush with the vertical surface of the hill.

At first, Clint thought it was another cave that didn't lead much of anywhere. Most of the ones he and George had been exploring were barely large enough to be used as an animal's den. Squinting into the darkness, Clint hollered George's name. The echo that came back to him let Clint know that this was one of the bigger caves they'd found. Once his eyes became adjusted to the shadows after being in the sun for so long, he saw a wide enclosed space that narrowed down into what looked to be a passage several yards farther inside.

In response to his voice, a dim light bobbed a ways down that passage. "That you, Clint?" George shouted.

"No, it's a bunch of robbers who know your name and where to find you. Of course it's me!"

When George finally stuck his head around a corner so Clint could see it, he showed that the passage wasn't as deep as it had originally seemed. The grin on his face could have been spotted from a mile away. "Glad you're back! That means you must've put that killer down for good, right?"

"I couldn't find him," Clint said as he ventured into the cave. The ceiling was jagged and uneven. Every step he took brought him into tighter quarters. The walls pinched in on him from both sides, making him quickly feel as if he was trapped in an upright coffin. "Whoever that fellow was, he wasn't the sort to just charge in. He'd send his men in for that, but he struck me as a careful sort."

George's enthusiastic smile faded when he heard that and nearly disappeared when he asked, "So that one careful fellow just disappeared?"

"No, but you rode those trails," Clint said. "They wind all over the damn place. I caught sight of him a few times, but by the time I made any headway, he disappeared around a bend or maybe even found someplace to duck in and hide."

George stayed put until Clint managed to squeeze through the narrow passage. On the other end of it, the cave widened out again and led to a sharp corner that was currently illuminated by the small lantern in George's hand. "I suppose we proved we could handle ourselves well enough. Maybe he won't even want to tangle with us again."

"Yeah," Clint said. "I found that one man who came after you. Made a real mess of him, didn't you?"

"Truth is," George muttered, "I was trying to get to my horse. I heard him coming as soon as I took a few steps and fired." He shrugged. "Hit a rock and the man fell over screaming. Must've been a ricochet."

"Told you those could be deadly."

"He was still gonna shoot me so—"

"You finished him off."

George nodded. "Seemed a cowardly way to kill a man."

"There aren't a lot of great ways to kill a man," Clint told him. "It was him or you so you didn't have another choice. Doesn't mean you have to like it."

Judging by the haunted expression on his face, George hadn't shot many other men. Since George had the rest of his life to dwell on that moment, Clint decided to steer him away from it for now. "You seemed mighty happy when I first came in here," he said. "What did you find?"

George's face brightened again. "Actually, I just got a look at it myself, and let me tell you, it's pretty damn impressive."

"More gold?"

"Gold and . . . well . . . come have a look for yourself." Without waiting for a response, George turned his back to Clint and carefully navigated the passage.

"How could anyone drag anything into this damned place?" Clint grunted. "I can barely tell up from down."

"Must've taken a few trips, but you have to admit this is a good place to hide something. The path alone discourages a man from getting all the way to the end."

When Clint rounded the next sharp corner, he found himself face to face with George. "Christ almighty. What possessed you to follow that damn tunnel?"

"I don't know," George replied while turning around to walk even farther into it. "But I'm sure glad I did."

When George swung around to shine the light where it was needed, Clint saw even more than he'd been expecting.

"This has got to be one of the larger stores," George said.

There was a small barrel nearby, which he used as a table for the lantern. That way, he could angle it toward the small wooden boxes stacked toward the back of the cave a few yards away. "Look at it in there," he sighed through a greedy smirk.

Clint could see the sparkle of gold between the slats of those boxes at the back of the cave, but something else had caught his eye. "Get that lantern off of that!" he snapped.

"What? You mean the barrel?"

"It's not a barrel, you idiot. It's a goddamn powder keg."

George turned around so quickly that he almost knocked the lantern over. Fortunately, he kept himself just steady enough to pick up the lantern and lower it so he could get a closer look for himself. "You're right. How'd you know?"

"I can smell the gunpowder. There's a whole lot more in here than just gold."

"I'll say. This could be a mother lode!"

Apart from what they'd already found, there was plenty more stored in the depths of all that rock. The goods stacked along the walls were covered by dusty tarps. Clint walked over to one of them to pull it off, already forming a good idea of what he would find. When he saw the short row of rifles propped against the wall beneath the tarp, he nodded slowly.

"Guns?" George said. "Why would anyone store guns way out here?"

"These look to be more than the weapons you could find at a store in town."

"Look like a bunch of rifles to me."

"That's because you don't know any better." Clint picked one up to get a closer look. As soon as he felt the weight of it in his hands and the tension in the firing mechanism, he said, "Bring that lantern over here."

George stepped over to him, but slowly angled the light toward the smaller boxes and their glittering contents.

"Keep it here where I can see," Clint told him.

"What is it? Is that a valuable weapon?"

"It cost a pretty penny to have it made."

"Really?" George asked. "How do you know?"

"Because I'm the one who made it."

THIRTEEN

"How do you know that one's yours?"

Clint turned the rifle in his hands so he could look at it from several different angles. "This wasn't just some rifle. It was a custom order. The man who ordered it wanted it modified to fire a higher caliber round. There were also changes to be made for it to send that round farther and with more accuracy."

"No offense, Clint, but it would seem to make more sense just to buy a different rifle than gussy one up."

"Custom rifles like this one are higher quality and are worth a whole lot more."

"How much more?" George asked.

"Bring that lantern closer."

This time, George was eager to comply.

"That doesn't look like a fancy rifle," George said. "Looks like a piece of trash. Uh . . . I'm sure it looked fine when you first worked on it but—"

"Do me a favor," Clint said. "Hang that lantern."

After a few seconds of fumbling, the lantern swung from a spot only slightly above their eye level.

"Why are you still looking at that rifle?"

"This is another one that was under the same tarp. Same modifications."

"Could it have been someone else who did the work on them?"

"No," Clint replied with certainty. "I remember working on these. Damn fine job, if I do say so myself."

Standing over by the smaller boxes in the back of the cramped space, George pried one open with his bare hands so he could shove his fingers inside and scoop out a bunch of coins.

"Wait a second," he said. "These are the same coins as the others we found. And if they're part of the Preston fortune, that means those rifles belonged to Preston, too."

Clint was still examining the rifle in his hands. He brought it closer to the lantern so he could get a better look at a portion of the stock that was splintered and cracked.

"Don't you see?" George asked impatiently.

"See what?"

"These rifles must have belonged to Preston . . . or at least someone close to the Prestons. And if you're the one who built them . . ."

"Actually, I just modified them," Clint said.

"Whatever," George said. "My point is that you must have met up with at least one of the Prestons!"

Clint asked, "So what if I did?"

"Then perhaps you know some places where they preferred to go. Perhaps someplace that was safe enough for you to work." George snapped his fingers. "Where did they meet with you to commission the job you did on those rifles? Do you remember who you spoke to? Was it in Texas?"

"Do me a favor."

Nodding excitedly, George replied, "Yeah? What?"

"Cool your heels on this and let me get a look at these rifles in the daylight. For now, let's start carrying some of these boxes out of here."

As Clint had hoped, the mention of looting the cave was more than enough to distract George's attention. "I was thinking one of us could stay here and the other can go back to the entrance. That way, we each only have to walk half the length of that damn tunnel."

"Fine. I'll take the second part of the chain and bring what you hand me into the main portion of the cave."

"Why?" George asked as he narrowed his eyes into slits. "You think I'll ride off and leave you here if I'm the one closest to the horses?"

Clint let out a haggard sigh. "We've come this far around so much gold without nipping at each other. Let's not start now. It's too damn hot and I'm too damn tired for it."

The suspicious expression on George's face quickly shifted to one of embarrassment. "You're right, Clint. Sorry about that."

"If you want to switch places, be my guest."

And in the blink of an eye, George's embarrassed expression snapped right back into the more familiar enthusiastic one. "That sounds like a great plan. Let's get started."

Clint wasn't about to argue with that. The first thing he did was squeeze his way back through the winding tunnel that brought him back to where the horses were waiting. As soon as he poured some water from his canteen into a large groove in the floor, both horses lapped it up gratefully. He then secured their reins as best he could before working his way through the tunnel once again. Fortunately, he only needed to go halfway this time.

After scraping through the same tunnel several times in a row, Clint stopped feeling every bump and bruise. The repetition also made the trip seem shorter each time. After a few hours, George shuffled all the way down the passage to meet Clint at the front of the cave.

As soon as he got a look at his partner in the brighter light, George removed his hat and used the back of his hand to mop the sweat from his brow. "Damn! Do I look half as bad as you?"

George's face was filthy and streaked with slender lines of blood from spots where his scalp had been introduced to the cave wall. His shirt was torn and the portion of his arms that were revealed by the sleeves he'd rolled up were battered, bloodied, and bruised.

Glancing down at his own forearms to find them similarly abused, Clint winced to feel plenty of sore spots on his face. "I imagine we're both worse for wear."

"Yeah," George said as he sat down on a pile of narrow boxes containing the gold coins. "But at least we got everything out of there." He looked around at the stacks Clint had made. There were two short piles of rifles, a few small crates of dynamite, and just over a dozen of the narrow boxes containing the real apple of George's eye. It didn't seem to be as much as when it was all crammed into a smaller room, but that wasn't George's main concern.

"Wait a minute," he said. "How the hell are we going to get all of this stuff back to town?"

Clint smirked and helped himself to what was left of his water. "I was wondering when you were going to ask that. There's way too much to be carried by two horses, especially when they need to ride over this kind of terrain. Add in the heat and dryness of the air and you're looking at several trips back and forth. Unless . . ."

George suddenly blinked and perked up. "A wagon!"

"There you go."

"You could have mentioned something to me as I kept handing you those boxes."

"I could have. I just didn't want you to slow down on account of you sulking from lack of planning."

"Truth be told, I didn't think we'd find so much. Now that we have . . ."

"Now that we have," Clint said, "we'll need a wagon. Surely you can get one back in town."

George nodded. "I know where to rent one."

"Then you go and rent it. I'll stay here to guard the gold."

George gnashed his teeth. "You think those men will come back?"

"Those men or possibly others. There's a chance that these caves were chosen by Preston or whoever because there's no fast way in or out. It takes time to raid this stash."

"Enough time for reinforcements to be sent."

Clint nodded. "Now you're thinking. If you're worried about me riding off as soon as you leave . . ."

George stopped him with a quick wave. "If you wanted to double-cross me, you would have shot me by now."

"Or I could wait until the gold's loaded onto the wagon."

Shrugging, George said, "Either way, it's got to be loaded. I'm sick of this damn desert and I'm doubly sick of this cave. Let's get this done and worry about the rest later."

FOURTEEN

The main thing that seemed to be working in Clint's favor at the moment was the fact that they'd gotten such an early start to their day. George had been gone long enough that he must have made it back into town already. Judging by how anxious he was, George could very well have found the cart he was after and started back into the desert. It would be some time before the wagon made it back to the caves, but Clint figured they could get it loaded and on its way back before it was too dark to travel. In the meantime, he had plenty to keep him busy.

As soon as he'd rested for a spell, Clint picked up the rifle that he'd carried with him when he'd left the store-room at the back of the cave. It was the rifle that had first caught his eye, and now that he could see it in the light of day, it was easy enough to recognize his own handiwork. The rifle had been built a few years ago, and when he disassembled it to examine each modification that had been made, he winced and shook his head.

"Looks like I put this one together with my eyes closed," he grumbled.

If he'd seen the same craftsmanship on anyone else's work, he would have appreciated it more. Since it was his own, however, he saw every last imperfection before noticing any of the finer points. He didn't need to scrutinize the rifle for long before the memories began to flow from the back of his mind up to the front, where they could be seen again. Once he'd recalled what he could of putting the rifle together, Clint focused on the damage that had been done to it in the years that had followed.

The stock was cracked after being smashed against a rock or possibly crushed after a fall. When he'd first seen the rifle, Clint thought sections of the barrel were rusted. Now that he had more light, he could see that it wasn't rust after all. Rust didn't scrape off so easily. Clint looked at the thumb he'd used to do the scraping, rubbed the dark flakes between his fingers, and then sniffed them carefully.

"Blood," he said. Looking at the rifle the way a doctor might look at a patient, he said, "What the hell happened to you?"

He then turned his attention to the other rifles. Two of them just needed a good cleaning, but the rest were just as bad or even worse than the first one he'd found. Some had bent barrels that could have been trampled beneath a wagon. Others had damage on their stocks that had definitely been put there by gunfire. Nearly all of them were stained with at least a small amount of blood.

"Well," he said after setting the last rifle aside, "at least none of them suffered from a misfire."

Clint picked another of the rifles at random and disassembled that one. When he examined the parts this time, he looked for signs of how well the rifle had been maintained, how many times it had been fired, and what sort of punishment it had been given. Any gunsmith worth his salt would have been able to tell the rifle had been put through its paces. Since he knew the sort of material he'd used and the quality of the craftsmanship, Clint guessed the rifle had been fired enough times to have been through a war.

"Preston," he said to himself. "Preston." When he looked over to Eclipse, Clint said, "Do you remember someone named Preston?"

The Darley Arabian was used to Clint talking to him every now and then, but didn't have any answers for him.

"I know I've met a few Prestons over the years, but not the sort of men that George is talking about." As he spoke to put his thoughts in order, Clint went through the process of putting the rifles back together again. It was a set of motions that were second nature to him and never failed to act as a sort of comfort. No matter what else was going on or what sort of chaos was around him, a rifle fit together in the same manner. There weren't many things that remained so constant.

Clint continued airing out his thoughts. "Jebediah Preston. Jeb. *El General*. The General. A few years ago . . . What? A major? A captain? Hell, for all I know, the rank is just something he gave to himself."

Having completed one rifle, Clint reached for the next one. That weapon's barrel slipped from his fingers to clang against the stone floor.

"Stone," he whispered. "That's it! Not Major. Martin. Martin Stone! I'll be damned."

And in a rush, the memories started to flow through Clint's mind.

FIFTEEN

Martin Stone was a proud Texan. When Clint was introduced to him, the first thing that stood out was his perfectly
trimmed silvery gray hair and piercing eyes. Like many
rich men, he carried himself as if anyone in his sight was
beneath him. Somehow, he had enough charm to offset
that. Of course, the generous fees he was willing to pay
for Clint's time went a long way in that regard.

The spread near San Antonio was supposed to be a ranch,
but it struck Clint as something closer to a small village.
There were several houses on the middle of the property
and several small businesses out toward the periphery. There
was a blacksmith, a hotel, and even a saloon.

Clint was there on business of his own. So far, that business seemed to be going very well.

"This," Martin Stone said as he held the modified rifle
in front of him, "is some damn fine work."

"Thanks, Mr. Stone, but it's really nothing too special."

"You shouldn't be so modest, and please . . . call me Martin."

Sitting in a padded chair in the middle of all that sprawling Texas property with a glass of expensive whiskey in his hand, Clint wasn't about to disagree. "Sure thing, Martin. I heard you were looking for rifles."

Martin took his seat behind a mahogany desk and set the rifle down onto a cloth that had been rolled out like a placemat. Placing a set of spectacles upon the bridge of his nose, he leaned down to study the weapon some more. "Who told you I wanted rifles?" he asked.

"Fella in San Antonio by the name of Roth."

"Ben Roth," Martin said without looking up from the rifle in front of him. "He's one of my representatives."

"That explains why he told me to come here," Clint replied.

"He also should have told you I was interested in selling several rifles I have in my possession so I could purchase newer ones."

"He did. According to your representative, you want rifles that can punch a hole through a man with better accuracy at two hundred yards."

"That's right," Martin replied.

"That rifle there should be able to do the job from around two hundred and fifty yards," Clint told him. "Farther if the man firing it knows what he's doing."

Martin shifted his eyes to look at Clint over the wire rim of his spectacles. "I can't even tell what sort of rifle this is."

"Started out as a .44 carbine. Now it packs a little more punch. If you don't like that, I can knock the caliber up a bit more. Of course, I'll have to make the ammunition myself, but that's not a problem."

"Why would I want that as opposed to purchasing newer rifles that suit my purpose?" Martin asked.

"Because whatever you buy won't suit your purposes better than that rifle right there."

Martin placed both hands flat upon his desk and sat up straight. After a few seconds, he removed the spectacles from his nose, put them into a case, and reached out to open a finely carved wooden box. "When I start into business with someone for the first time, I like to have a cigar. Do you care for one, Mr. Adams?"

"That's why I'm here."

"Then you'll bring your price down."

"How far?"

Martin said, "Half."

Clint set his whiskey glass down and stood up. "I appreciate your time. Guess I'll be on my way."

Martin only lifted one hand, but it was enough to get Clint to stop where he was. "Do you sell guns or just fix them?"

"I'm a gunsmith. I can repair a broken firearm. That," Clint said while pointing down to the rifle on Martin's desk, "isn't just a repair. That is a special order and I dare you to find one that fires any better."

"I suppose this is something you sell often?"

"I made it special," Clint replied. "And I can make more if you're interested."

"How big of an order can you fill?"

"As long as I've got the parts and as long as the price is enough to justify the time I'll be spending, I can fill any order you need. Within reason, of course."

Martin picked up the rifle, felt the weight in his hands, and worked the lever. Every mechanism on the weapon moved as smooth as silk. Despite the fact that he was in the middle of a negotiation, Martin couldn't keep himself from nodding in appreciation of the fine craftsmanship on display. "Does your price include the cost of the parts you'll need?"

"That's the best part," Clint told him. "That rifle in front of you was made from some of the rifles your man in San Antonio was looking to sell."

Anger showed upon Martin's face. "How many of my guns did he hand over to you?"

"Two," Clint replied. "But I bought them. Those parts, combined with some I brought along with me and my own skill in the trade, made that weapon."

Clint hadn't done many special orders in a while, and when he'd heard about Martin Stone, he'd become inspired.

Hearing that he hadn't lost on the deal soothed Martin's nerves somewhat. "You bought a few of the guns he was selling just so you could take them apart, piece them back together again, and sell them back to me?"

"That's what I do. The point being, if I were to piece together custom rifles for you, the parts would be an additional expense. You've already got most of the parts I'd need to fill the order your man in San Antonio was asking about."

"So if I didn't have the parts, your fee would be even higher?" Martin leaned back as if he was recovering from a glancing right cross to the nose. "I sincerely hope you're not taking me for a fool, Adams."

"Not at all. My services don't come cheap. I've done plenty of business with plenty of folks. There's a man up in West Texas who can answer any questions you might have about me."

"I prefer to see things for myself."

Clint leaned forward with both hands flat on top of Martin's desk. "Then take that rifle and put it to the test against any other you want to buy around here. If you find something better, let me know and I'll be on my way."

"How about you stay here as my guest," Martin offered. "There are clean rooms in the saloon and the bar stocks the best beer and liquor you're likely to find outside of Dallas."

"What about the restaurant? Do they serve a good steak?"

"Best damn cut of beef in Texas," Martin said without hesitation. "Spend a few days here. Your room and board will be seen to, as will your horse."

Now it was Clint's turn to study the man across from him. "That's a whole lot of generosity. What's the catch?" he asked.

"This weapon looks very nice," Martin said while patting the rifle on his desk. "But I'm no expert. I want to have some of my men take a look at it and I'd like you to stay put while they do. If they like what they see, perhaps you can put another one together so they can make sure you can deliver on an entire order. As for the catch," he added with a shrug, "let's just say it's a return on the investment you already made. You purchased a few of my rifles, took the time to modify them, and used some of your own parts to do so. I'm keeping this rifle in exchange for my hospitality while you're here. Does that seem like a fair deal?"

Considering the fact that many in San Antonio considered Martin Stone to be the richest man in southern Texas, Clint didn't have much trouble in agreeing to that proposition.

"I think I can stay put for a day or two," Clint said.

"It shouldn't take any longer than that for me to see what I need to make a decision."

"Then you've got yourself a deal."

"Excellent. I'll have someone show you around."

SIXTEEN

When Clint stepped out of Martin's house, a skinny man with sunken cheeks and age spots on his scalp where hair used to be was standing outside to meet him.

"You'd be Mr. Adams?" the old-timer asked.

"I am."

"I'm Bass. I'm to show you to the livery and point you in the direction of anything else you might need."

"Lead the way," Clint said.

The livery wasn't far from the house and was fairly impressive in its own right. It was easily double the size of a regular stable with a pair of fancy carriages inside already. Since just over half of the horse stalls were full, Clint knew there had to be other stables nearby.

"You need anything special done for you?" Bass asked.

"No, thanks."

The old man stepped closer to him and dropped his voice to a conspiratorial whisper. "If there's anything that does need doing, might as well ask. Mr. Preston don't ask no questions, this bein' his private livery."

"Mr. Preston?"

"Sure. He owns the land and plenty of what's on it."

Clint shrugged and said, "I'd just like to make certain my horse is well cared for."

"Oh, that goes without sayin'. You hungry?"

"Nothing tastes better than a free steak."

"I hear ya!" Bass led the way out of the stable.

As soon as they stepped outside, Clint spotted one of the prettier sights he'd seen since he'd arrived. She was a smiling brunette waiting for them with hands resting upon full, rounded hips. Dressed like any one of the cowboys working on the ranch, she wore dusty jeans and a faded cotton shirt that clung to a generous figure.

"What are you two doing?" she asked, smiling.

"I was just about to give Mr. Adams here the tour," Bass replied. "Figured we'd stop off at Miss Millie's first for a bite to eat."

"Perfect," she said. "I'm famished."

"You're welcome to join us."

She stepped between the old man and Clint. "I have a better idea. Why don't I take over from here? Surely you've got better things to do."

"Sure," Bass said, "there's always something else that needs to be done, but I could always—"

"Great," she said before he could finish. "It's this way, Mr. Adams."

"Please," he said as he offered his arm to her, "call me Clint."

She took his arm and fell into step beside him with a bounce that was impossible for Clint to miss. Her skin had the dark color acquired from spending most of her days in the sun, and her lips were naturally full and red.

"How do you do, Clint? I'm Felicia."

"Pleased to meet you. Either this is my lucky day or this town has the best welcoming committee in Texas."

"The committee depends on who needs to be welcomed," she replied. "Usually it's just a bunch of cowboys or some of my grandfather's business associates. You don't strike me as either."

"Who's your grandfather?"

"Martin Stone."

"Then I hate to disappoint you," Clint said with an exaggerated wince. "I do have business with him."

She stuck out her bottom lip in a well-practiced pout, which definitely had its desired effect on him. "Usually I'm so good at judging the men that come through here."

"Obviously you've sized me up. Tell me what you guessed and I'll let you know how close you are."

"I pegged you as someone passing through here on your way to make a fortune. Probably some big, risky venture or maybe even something dangerous."

"Does every man who rides through here seem dangerous?"

"Most of those men don't wear a gun on their hip. At least," she was quick to add, "they don't look like they're as comfortable with a gun as you do."

"Then perhaps you should look closer," Clint said. "Any man who wants to keep healthy tends to go heeled when riding on their own."

"But they're not all Clint Adams, now are they?"

He smiled and nodded. "So you had me pegged even better than I expected."

"Some of the ranch hands mentioned your name. And I'd heard about you a time or two before then."

"Nothing bad, I hope."

"It wasn't all good," she said with a grin. "Lots of our cattle are driven down through West Texas. When those men get back, they usually have lots of stories to tell. More than a few of them involve you."

"I see," Clint said. "I guess it could have been worse. What did you hear exactly?"

"Enough to catch my interest," she replied. "What brings you here?"

"One of the less exciting things I do is ply my trade as a gunsmith. I doubt that gets mentioned in those stories you heard." And after a long losing streak at the poker tables, Clint had needed to take some time off. Of course, there was no reason to bother a pretty lady with details.

Looking around at the shops nearby, she asked, "Are we getting our very own gunsmith?"

"Not on a permanent basis. I heard about an opportunity while I was in San Antonio. It seems Mr. Stone is looking to put together a small group of regulators to patrol his property and he needs to make sure they've got the tools for the job."

Felicia rolled her eyes. "I hope it's not just another bunch of damn fools with big mouths strutting around here."

"From what I've already seen of your grandfather, I don't think he'd cut corners with the men he hires."

"Maybe he'll hire you."

"Maybe."

"Don't you want to stay on for a while?" she asked. "If you like, I could put a good word in on your account."

"Why don't I just take one job at a time? I haven't even been given a firm offer on the rifles yet."

"I wouldn't worry too much about that."

Clint laughed. "Don't put too much stock to those stories you've heard about me."

"I don't," she assured him. "I fully intend to size you up for myself from every possible angle."

Although Felicia was more than enough to hold any man's attention, something else caught Clint's eye as he was escorted to a place named Millie's Cook House. Two men stood in front of a general store with their arms crossed and scowls on their faces. The scowls didn't concern Clint as much as the way they stared while speaking quietly to each other.

The smaller of the two turned his back to Clint and walked inside the store. The second man held his ground.

"Who are they?" Clint asked.

Felicia was just about to open the front door to Millie's when she stopped to look back at him. "Who?"

"Those two across the street. Well, there's only one now, but there were two just a moment ago."

She spotted the man with the intense glare right away. "Oh, that's Cal Landry. He watches out for my grandfather's interests. He'll probably be one of the men firing those rifles of yours."

"The other man was tall, broad shoulders, dark skin."

"That'd be John VanTreaton. He does the same sort of work as Cal, but isn't such an asshole about it."

"Any reason why either of those men would be watching me like that?" Clint asked.

"My grandfather takes his business seriously. He probably sent them to keep an eye on you."

Clint had a few more questions, but they left his mind when he got a whiff of the steaks cooking inside Millie's. Across the street, Cal followed in John's footsteps by entering the general store. Whoever they were or whatever they wanted, Clint knew he'd find out soon enough. Besides, Felicia was much more inviting to him as she led the way into Millie's with her hips swaying nicely.

SEVENTEEN

For Clint, dinner was just fine and the company was even better. Felicia sat across from him, watching him with eyes that promised one hell of a memorable dessert. He was so looking forward to tasting it that he nearly didn't see the ax handle that was swung directly at his face.

Clint reacted out of reflex without even knowing what was coming his way. His first thought was to duck and let whatever it was sail over his head. He might have done just that if Felicia hadn't been directly behind him. Instead, he reached up with both hands to catch the incoming swing. Clint had guessed the tall man meant to punch him, so he was mighty surprised when the solid wooden ax handle slapped against both of his palms.

"Son of a bitch!" Clint growled in response to the painful surprise.

Although the impact stung like hell, Clint was able to stop the swing dead in its tracks. He tightened his grip on the ax handle and turned toward the man who'd swung it. John VanTreaton glared right back at him. When the dark-skinned man tried to reclaim his weapon, he pulled Clint along with it.

"John!" Felicia hollered. "What are you doing?"

VanTreaton didn't seem to hear her as he bared his teeth and continued to try and take back the ax handle.

Using all the strength he could muster, Clint pulled the ax handle in one direction. When VanTreaton shifted his weight to respond, Clint pulled in the opposite direction while twisting the handle around as sharply as he could. Between the jarring change of direction and the painful way his wrists were strained, VanTreaton wasn't able to hold on to his weapon very long. Clint didn't have much time to celebrate, however, before the other man's head snapped forward.

VanTreaton's skull thumped against the bridge of Clint's nose right between his eyes. He'd heard boxers talk about getting their bell rung, and moments like this made it painfully clear what they meant. For a moment, Clint could hear nothing apart from a dull thrumming, and he staggered as if the floor were being tilted beneath his feet. He recovered after a heartbeat or two, but crumpled a bit more as if he was still reeling.

"You ain't nothing," VanTreaton snarled as he raised the ax handle high above his head.

Not only was Clint feigning how hurt he was, but he'd also shifted all of his weight to his back foot without VanTreaton taking much notice. Now that the larger man had both of his arms raised, he presented Clint with a nice, big target. Clint pushed himself forward to slam his shoulder into the other man's midsection. Even after they collided, Clint continued churning his feet beneath him to drive VanTreaton as far back as he could.

As soon as he could tell he was charging toward a wall, Clint used the rest of his momentum to shove the other man back. VanTreaton hit the wall solidly and expelled a good portion of his wind in one huffing grunt. Clint knew better than to stop there. He immediately started hammering away at VanTreaton's stomach with a series of quick punches. His knuckles pounded against what felt like a side of beef, so Clint raised his aim a bit.

VanTreaton's head snapped back when he caught Clint's uppercut on the chin. He responded by bringing the ax handle into Clint's ribs with a short, chopping blow. Clint twisted away, moving his sore ribs back and out of the other man's reach.

"What the hell are you after?" Clint asked.

Without saying a word, VanTreaton took a swing at Clint with the ax handle. If Clint didn't lean back at just the right time, the piece of carved wood might have knocked his head clean off his shoulders.

"Clint," Felicia said from the doorway. "Cal is nearby."

"Of course he is," Clint said with a grin meant to ruffle VanTreaton's feathers. "This one here wouldn't go too far on his own. That might just put him into something close to a fair fight."

VanTreaton didn't like that one bit, and he made it known by swinging at Clint a few more times. Each time was a downward attack as if he were driving a railroad spike into the ground. Clint sidestepped one and then the other before snapping a quick right hook into VanTreaton's chin. The larger man barely seemed to feel the punch before driving one end of the ax handle into Clint's gut again.

When Clint saw his next opening, he didn't waste time with another hook or jab. Instead, he clasped both hands together as if he had a club of his own. Even though he wasn't brandishing a weapon, his fists made a jarring impact when they thumped against VanTreaton's elbow. It was the closest target Clint could reach. Even if it didn't do a lot of damage, VanTreaton wasn't able to take another swing of his own right away. Clint put the extra second he'd bought to good use by bashing his fists into the other man's jaw.

VanTreaton staggered back half a step and shook his head before spitting out a juicy wad of blood. "You . . . ain't nothing."

Despite the fact that he was still up and talking, VanTreaton was taking a moment to catch his breath. Clint took a moment as well to look around at who else was watching the fight. Felicia was still standing by the front door, and a few others were scattered here and there just to take in the spectacle. It took less than a second for Clint to spot Cal standing across the street.

"What's the matter?" Clint shouted toward Cal. "You're not going to lend your partner a hand?"

"Don't think he needs one," Cal replied.

When Clint turned back toward VanTreaton, he found the dark-skinned man already cocking his arm back for another swing with the ax handle. In a smooth motion, Clint drew his modified Colt and fired a shot. Smoke curled from the Colt's barrel as chips flew from the tip of the ax handle. Clint squeezed his trigger again, driving another bullet through the length of wood about halfway down. He paused for half a second, fired again, and chopped the ax handle into two pieces.

Once the top portion of the handle hit the ground, Clint asked, "What about now? Think he needs any help?"

VanTreaton took a moment to examine the broken end of the ax handle before looking across the street.

Cal stayed where he was. Both hands hung at his sides within easy reach of his holstered pistol.

"That's enough of this!" Felicia said. "All three of you!"

"I didn't start this mess," Clint told her.

"But you're about to make it a whole lot worse if you shoot anyone."

"Where my next bullet goes is up to these two here."

With the snap of his wrist, VanTreaton threw the piece of his ax handle with enough force for the splintered end to stick into the ground near Clint's feet. He glared at Clint, let out a single huffing breath, and walked away. Cal followed suit a second later.

"What was that all about?" Clint asked.

Felicia approached him and said, "I don't know, but it's over."

Somehow, Clint doubted that.

EIGHTEEN

Clint rented a room above the smaller of the two saloons on the property. Any similarities the ranch had to a town stopped when it came to keeping the peace. After Clint's scuffle with VanTreaton and Landry, the only keepers of the peace to come around were a few ranch hands armed with shotguns. Once they saw the fight was over, they shrugged and headed into the largest saloon.

The room Clint rented was strictly bare bones. There was a bed, a stack of linens, a table, and a wash basin. Despite the lack of any other niceties, Clint was happy to get off his feet. As soon as his backside hit the edge of the mattress, he began tugging at his boots.

"Thanks for the tour of the place," he said. "Hope you don't mind showing yourself out."

Felicia stepped inside and shut the door. "I'm doing nothing of the sort. You could use some tending."

"What I can use the most is some sleep. Anything else will have to wait for a while."

She waved that away like his refusal was a fly buzzing around her head. "Stop your grousing and let me help you."

"Grousing? Didn't you see that big fellow trying to knock my head off my shoulders?"

"He didn't, did he?" she said.

"Well . . . no."

"Then you'll be fine. Here, let me lend you a hand."

Since she wanted to lend a hand with peeling his shirt off, Clint allowed her to do so. Once she'd removed his shirt, she went to the water basin and dipped a small cloth into it. Felicia returned to the bed and crawled on it to sit behind Clint. The water was cold and Clint flinched when he felt the cloth touch his side.

"Good Lord, you're fidgety!" she said.

"Just try not to scrub a spot that wasn't already pummeled by that big ox."

"How about this?" Felicia asked as she used the cloth to dab at a spot on the side of Clint's head that was caked with dried blood.

He tried to grit his teeth through his discomfort, but eventually brushed her hand away.

She sighed and placed her hand on a spot on his lower back that was dark from bruises. When Clint grunted and shifted uncomfortably, she threw the wet rag across the room. "There's just no pleasing you," she grumbled.

"You know what would please me?" Clint asked. "Let me get some sleep."

For a moment, Clint thought that she was about to surrender and let him have what he'd requested. Felicia was moving a bit behind him, but not much. Instead of climbing down off the bed, she placed her hands softly on his shoulders and leaned forward to whisper in his ear.

"How about this?" she asked. "Is that better for your delicate sensibilities?"

"My sensibilities don't have a thing to do with it," he replied. "I'm just tired."

He could feel the heat of her body behind him. When she started to gently rub his shoulders, he closed his eyes and savored the touch of her soft hair brushing against his neck.

"That's nice," he said.

"Yeah?"

Clint nodded and reached over his shoulder to touch her cheek. Felicia turned her head toward him so he could feel her full lips followed by the flicker of her tongue against his fingers. Soon she dragged her fingers lightly down his back and slipped her arms around him so she could rub his chest.

"You like this?" she whispered.

Not only could Clint feel her hands massaging his chest, but she leaned against him from behind so he could feel the warm, soft flesh of her breasts pressing against him. He smiled and said, "I like that very much."

Her hands wandered down the front of his body but couldn't quite reach all the way to his groin. Clint twisted around to find that she had indeed stripped out of her shirt. Felicia's firm breasts stood proudly on display, capped with dark nipples that were fully erect. He cupped one of them in his hand and placed his other hand on her hip.

Felicia smiled and kissed him. Soon, Clint felt her hands push against his chest with enough force to shove him onto his back. He allowed himself to be brought down, but he tried to sound stern when he asked, "What do you think you're doing?"

"If you don't know," she replied while stripping him out of his jeans, "then some of the things I've heard about you aren't exactly accurate." She continued to undress him until he lay naked on the bed. Staring hungrily down at his erect penis, she licked her lips and said, "I see some things about you are even better than I expected."

Clint ran his fingers through her thick dark hair as she lowered her head between his legs. She opened her mouth and wrapped her thick, full lips around his cock. As she took him into her mouth, Felicia ran her tongue on him, savoring every last inch. As she eased her head up, she teased his shaft with the tip of her tongue before climbing down from the bed.

"You better not be through," he told her.

To that, she merely grinned while peeling off every last stitch of her clothing. Felicia's body was taut and muscular, yet curvy in all the right places. When she crawled back onto the bed, she moved like a cat, digging her nails into the sheets while she lowered her head to lick any part of Clint that was within her reach.

He lay back and watched as she slowly mounted him. Her breasts swayed invitingly, and as soon as she'd straddled his hips, he reached up to cup them in both hands. Felicia let out a soft moan and moved her hips slowly. Although Clint wasn't inside her just yet, he could feel the slick lips of her pussy sliding against his rigid member. The more she moved, the wetter she got. All she needed to do from there was reach down and guide him to the right spot so he could slip inside her.

When Clint impaled her, both of them moaned in a mixture of relief and satisfaction. Felicia settled on top of him and placed both hands flat against his body to brace herself. When she saw the involuntary wince on Clint's face, she said, "Oops. Sorry about that. Still tender?"

"A bit, but I'll manage."

NINETEEN

"Here. I'm supposed to be taking care of you, remember?"

Felicia sat up straight and started to rock her hips back and forth. From that angle, Clint looked up at her and was able to see every line of her tight stomach and large breasts. Since he could no longer reach them, she placed her own hands upon her tits and started rubbing them as she slowly rocked back and forth.

Clint placed his hands on her legs to feel her muscles working to keep her entire body moving. His cock was deep inside her, and when he pumped his hips up a bit more, she arched her back and started to moan even louder. Felicia put her hands on her knees and bounced up and down on top of him. Her pussy glided along the length of his shaft, and her breasts swayed to the rhythm of her body. Clint closed his eyes until she stopped and started climbing off him.

He didn't even have enough time to pull her back before she turned around and climbed on top of him again. This time, she straddled him so her back was pointed toward his face. Considering the smooth lines of her back and rounded buttocks, that wasn't a bad thing at all. Felicia fit his pole inside her once more and then leaned forward to grab Clint's legs. His erection drove even deeper into her, touching a spot inside her body that caused Felicia to tremble with delight.

Soon, she grunted wildly and gripped his thighs as if she was hanging on for dear life. Clint drove her even wilder when he thrust up into her like a piston. Her backside bobbed up and down, and Clint couldn't help himself from reaching down to grab on to it.

"Yes, Clint," she cried. "I'm going to . . ." Suddenly, every one of Felicia's muscles tensed as she was overpowered by her climax.

Clint pulled out of her and turned her over. Felicia lay on her back and spread her legs open wide so Clint could climb on top of her. She was still breathing heavily when he entered her again.

She arched her back, pressing her breasts against him. Clint could feel her erect nipples brushing against his chest as he thrust into her again and again. Felicia locked eyes with him and wrapped her legs around his waist. Burying his face against her neck, all of Clint's senses were filled with her. He breathed in her scent. He felt the sweat on her skin and the wet lips of her pussy grip his cock. Clint took hold of her hands, pinned them to the bed, and pounded into her with a building rhythm. He drove into her again and again until, with one final powerful thrust, he exploded inside her . . .

"I have a confession to make," she whispered.

"Let me guess," Clint sighed. "Your grandfather wanted you to soften me up so I'd either go for a deal that favors him or stay here as one of his hired hands."

Felicia sat up straight and looked at him with her mouth hanging open. "Why would you say such a thing?"

"Am I right or wrong?"

Reluctantly, she said, "You're right . . . but why would you say that?"

"Because there aren't a lot of other confessions you'd likely make right about now. I can think of a few, but they're long shots, and seeing as how Martin Stone is related to you and I'm here on business with him . . . it only makes sense." After thinking it over for a few seconds, Clint nodded. "Yeah. That's the only one that makes sense."

"Just so you know, he didn't tell me to . . . you know . . . do what we just did."

"Don't worry," Clint told her. "I don't mind being charmed in this instance. But you might be able to help me with one thing."

She turned back to him and stretched out on her stomach to use both hands to prop up her head. She kicked her feet back and forth in a way that drew his eye down to the muscular curves of her backside. "What is it?" she asked.

Clint got up and turned so he could rub her back. As soon as his hands found a tense spot between her shoulders, Felicia's entire body relaxed. "Have you ever heard of someone named Preston?"

"No."

"Are you sure?"

After letting out a slow breath that sounded more like a purr, she asked, "Are you trying to use your charms on me?"

"Do I need to?"

Turning to look over her shoulder at him, she studied Clint carefully. "Where did you hear that name?"

"From someone around here. I get the impression that it might be someone important. Maybe someone who works with your grandfather."

Felicia rolled onto her side, practically shoving Clint's hands away in the process. "Who mentioned that name to you? Why did it come up?"

"I just heard it in passing. It's probably nothing."

She obviously wanted to ask more questions, but bit her tongue for the moment. In that amount of time, Clint reversed his previous decision about ending the conversation.

"You've obviously heard the name before," he said. "Who's Preston?"

"Just someone that doesn't need to show his face around here," she replied while flopping onto her stomach and turning her face away from him.

"He does business with your grandfather?"

"Sometimes."

"Did he hurt you?"

She laughed once. It was more of a huffing breath before she said, "Not hardly."

Clint thought about it for a few moments and decided to let it drop. A man like Martin Stone would do business with plenty of folks, and a good number of them wouldn't be the most pleasant kind of people. In the end, Clint decided there wasn't much need to rock the boat.

Best to just wait and see what the next few days would bring. He stretched out and wrapped an arm around Felicia. She turned to face him, draped her leg over him, and pressed her warm body against his. There were certainly worse ways to spend a few days.

TWENTY

It was only a matter of hours before Clint found himself summoned to Martin Stone's office one more time. Unlike the last time he'd been escorted through the large house, Clint was greeted at the door by the man himself. On top of that, Martin Stone was eager to speak his piece.

"Come on in," Martin said. "Is there anything I can get for you? A whiskey perhaps?"

"I prefer beer if you have any."

The older man smiled widely. "The best in Texas!"

Clint was always amused by how many men claimed to have the best of whatever it was they were talking about. In Texas, those claims doubled.

After telling a young woman with pale skin to fetch the drinks, Martin strode through the house toward his inner sanctum. "I hear there was trouble. Some sort of altercation in front of one of the saloons?"

"They're two men who work for you," Clint replied. "And I'm sure you know all about it."

"Cal and VanTreaton. Yes, I did hear. I'd like to hear your side of things, though."

"There's not much to tell. I was being shown around when I saw them staring daggers at me from across the street. When I stepped outside a short while after that, VanTreaton tried to knock my skull into the next county."

"Terrible," Martin sighed.

"I defended myself and for some reason decided not to put a bullet through anyone's chest."

"You would have been well within your rights to take whatever action you deemed necessary."

"Don't you have any law around here?" Clint asked.

They'd reached Martin's office by now. Martin strode inside, walked around his desk, and motioned Clint toward one of the chairs in front of it. "Despite its size, this isn't a proper town. The shops and such that were built here are privately owned. Although county law still goes around here, we don't have the luxury of men on hand to enforce it. We're on our own."

"But that's the way you like it," Clint said. "Otherwise, I'm sure a man with your means could do something to change it."

Shrugging, Martin said, "I suppose you've got me there. Anyhow, I am truly grateful that nobody was hurt."

"Tell that to my ribs."

Martin smirked as if the whole matter was resolved. "You'll be glad to know that I've had some of my men look at that rifle you put together and they were all quite impressed. I'd like to place an order."

"That's good to hear."

"Then why do you seem disappointed?"

Clint leaned back in the chair and crossed his legs. "I suppose I'm just a little skeptical."

"I assure you my offer will be quite generous."

"It's not that. I'm more concerned with the fact that I nearly got knocked out of my boots by some of the men on your payroll and nothing is going to be done about it."

Martin's expression darkened somewhat. "There is the option to enforce the law ourselves. That's happened a few times in the past and it's never been pretty."

"I understand that much," Clint said. "What I still don't understand is why it happened at all."

"Who knows why some men do what they do? Perhaps," Martin added while steepling his fingers, "one or both of them were jealous about the time you were spending with my granddaughter."

"Or someone else didn't like it and decided to do something about it."

"Did any of them say anything to you? Anything at all that might tell you what happened? When I confront them about this embarrassment, I'd like to know everything I can."

Clint doubted anyone at all would be confronted with it after he left that office. "Nothing else to say, really. One of them came at me and I sent him hobbling away. Everything after that has been speculation. Guess I haven't really had much else to keep me occupied."

"You know what speculation gets you at the end of the day? Not a goddamn thing. I'd rather get down to business. That is, if that's all right with you."

"That's why I'm here."

On top of Martin's desk was a very familiar shape beneath a piece of brown fabric. Pulling aside the fabric like a magician at the end of a trick, Martin revealed the rifle that Clint had brought with him. "This," Martin said, "is a work of art."

Clint shrugged. "I do good work, but I don't know about art."

"Well, I know about guns, as do my men, and we all believe this to be some fine craftsmanship."

"You mentioned something about an offer?" Clint asked.

Martin grinned and nodded. "I want six of these beauties. I'm willing to pay handsomely. I've written out the details here." With that, Martin reached into a desk drawer and removed a small notebook. After opening it to the right page, he set the notebook down, turned it toward Clint, and slid it forward.

Clint took a moment to peruse the figures written neatly in ink. "There's money being offered here for more than just the rifles."

"That's right."

"What's this, a consultation fee?"

Leaning forward as if he hadn't already memorized every line of what he'd written, Martin said, "That's just a bonus given for indulging one of my men."

"Which one?" Clint asked.

"He's done work as a blacksmith. He's also the one who usually maintains the ranch's equipment. He'll be the one maintaining these rifles, so he'd like to be there when you assemble them."

It wasn't the first time that someone had wanted to try and replicate Clint's work. Considering how much was being offered, he wasn't about to get his nose bent too far out of shape. Besides, there was more to gunsmithing than just knowing what steps to follow. "Fine," Clint said while tearing the paper from the notebook and tucking it into his pocket. "I'll get started right away. With or without your blacksmith."

Martin got to his feet and offered his hand. As soon as Clint shook it, the older man placed that hand back down onto the rifle. "This truly is fine craftsmanship. It's not quite like any model I've seen. What's it called?"

"You're paying for it. Call it what you like."

"How about the Clint Adams Special? Seems appropriate."

"I'm sure one of your men will come up with something better."

TWENTY-ONE

The next few days were filled with work that Clint knew all too well. Some might have considered it boring to spend hours upon hours dismantling rifles, filing down some parts, reinforcing others, and hammering down new pieces to fit into place. It was slow, repetitive work that took place in a hot room filled with smoke. For Clint, it was a chance to clear his mind and get back to the simplest of all things.

It felt good to build. It felt even better to have a task in front of him that was familiar and even inviting. The tasks he needed to perform weren't exciting, but they allowed his hands to stay busy and a good, honest sweat to pour from his brow. It was the sort of work that had made him ply his trade in the first place. While he was wrapped up in it, he didn't need to worry about anything else. The only reminder he had of Martin Stone was when Clint spent time with Stone's granddaughter. During those nights, the old man was the last thing on Clint's mind.

The job wasn't one of his toughest ones. In fact, Clint could have been out of there in less time, but he needed to go slower in order for his observer to catch what he was doing. Whoever the fellow was, he wasn't much of a gun-smith. The way he watched every little thing Clint did, it seemed as if he'd barely handled a rifle before, let alone seen one in pieces on a workbench.

Clint didn't use any secret techniques when modifying the rifles. All he did was improve them using different methods that he'd picked up throughout the years. The rest was just practicing his craft. The other man watched like an eager student, occasionally trying to act as if he wasn't watching the process so he could do it himself later on. For Clint, once the deal had been struck and the first pay-ment made, it was just another job.

The moment he'd started in on the last rifle, Clint's silent observer went missing. It was late afternoon and Clint's hands were busy tinkering with the firing mecha-nism of an old Winchester. The job was so easy that he allowed his brain to wander. Mostly, he weighed the pros and cons of finishing the rifle as quickly as possible or getting one last night in a comfortable bed with Felicia.

Suddenly, the door to the workshop was pushed open and two men stomped inside. Clint looked over his shoul-der to find the observer and a man he hadn't seen before. The blacksmith who ran the shop where Clint was put to work came in last and shut the door behind him.

"Is this him?" the new arrival asked.

Before anyone could answer, Clint turned all the way around to face the trio. He held a hammer in one hand, which he propped on his shoulder while saying, "I don't much like it when folks pretend I'm not here. If you're talk-ing to me, step up and introduce yourself like a man."

The man Clint had never seen before cracked half a smile. He looked to be slightly younger than Clint, but that could have just been the product of good breeding. His thick hair was cut short in a manner that spoke of the

Federal Army almost as much as a crisp blue uniform. He wore a pistol on his hip. The confident way he kept his hand resting upon the grip told Clint that he would know how to put the weapon to work if the need arose.

"This here's Clint Adams," the observer said. At that moment, Clint felt a little strange for not knowing that man's name.

Acting as if he'd learned Clint's name from a passing breeze, the stranger ignored the observer completely and said, "I'm Allan Preston."

"Preston?" Clint replied. "I've heard mention of you."

"Did you? From who? The old man?"

"No. Mind if I ask what you're doing here?"

Preston looked at the other two men who'd walked in with him as if he couldn't decide which of them to slap. "I own this shop you're in," he said to Clint. "And I own a good portion of the land you're standing on."

"All right. That settles that. What can I do for you?"

Stepping forward, Allan asked, "Is that one of the rifles you were commissioned to make?"

"Yes sir, it is." When Allan reached for the largest piece of the dismantled rifle, Clint added, "That one's not finished yet."

"I can see that."

"If you want to examine a functioning model, I've got five others right over there."

Preston glanced in the direction Clint pointed and said, "Those rifles don't look the same."

"Strictly speaking, they're not," Clint said. "I put them together using parts from other rifles in Mr. Stone's possession. You can't just fit any parts together, though. They've had to be modified."

"Which is what you were hired to do."

"That's right."

Preston picked up the piece he'd originally reached for so he could take a closer look. After examining the firing mechanism as well as the barrel itself, he nodded and set them both down precisely as he'd found them. "That's some damn fine work."

"Glad you approve."

Swatting the observer with the back of his hand, Preston asked, "Do you think you could do work like that?"

"I've seen what he does," the observer replied. "It ain't much."

Clint sighed. "I've been hearing a lot of that lately."

"Well, whoever's saying that is wrong," Preston told him. "Seeing a man do something isn't the same as doing it yourself." He ran his hand over the top of his head while staring down at the dismantled rifle. He motioned toward the completed ones. "So the others are like this one?"

"Basically," Clint replied. "I did the same sort of modifications, but each one's going to be a little different. They should all measure up to the same quality as the sample I provided."

Preston reached into his pocket for a piece of folded paper. He unfolded it and then held it out so Clint could see. "Is this the list of modifications you made?"

Clint checked the list, but didn't have to look at it for long before he nodded. "That's right. Like I said, those five over there are ready to go and this one should be finished shortly."

"Sam," Preston said to the observer. "Collect those rifles that are finished. I want to make sure you at least know how to strip them down and put them together again."

"Christ almighty," Sam grumbled.

Knowing exactly how far under Sam's skin his words had dug, Preston grinned at Clint. "He likes to think of himself as a smith. Hopefully he's learned a thing or two."

"I am being paid extra," Clint pointed out. "I could answer any questions he has if he'd like to ask. Or . . . he could just keep hanging over me like a vulture."

"You're getting paid extra?" Preston asked.

"That's right."

Preston grinned, thought it over, and then grinned a little more. "Good," he said. "Soak the old man for every last penny."

At that moment, Clint decided to finish his work and be on his way before any more trouble came to that ranch.

TWENTY-TWO

OLD MEXICO
THE PRESENT . . .

George arrived just before nightfall with a covered wagon that had a wheel with a bent rim. Although the wagon suited their purposes just fine, it rattled like it was about to give up its ghost at any second. They were able to load the wagon and get down from the hills before losing too much daylight. If the rest of the ride hadn't been across relatively flat desert, they would have needed to make camp and go the rest of the way into town in the morning. As it was, the light from the stars was just enough to illuminate the plain of sandy rock until the town came into view.

Thanks to a deal already arranged with Ramon, George and Clint were able to unload the gold at the old miner's shop, where it would be held for safekeeping. After that, Clint barely managed to stay on his feet while shuffling toward his hotel.

"You can leave those with Ramon as well," George said.

Until that moment, Clint had almost forgotten he still

had a rifle in each hand. Glancing at the two weapons taken from the cave, Clint replied, "I still want to check a few things on these."

"You've had them most of the day. Haven't you seen all there is to see?"

"I've been doing some thinking and . . . I just want to check a few things over. Is that a problem?"

George waved a hand at him and started walking down the street. "Long as it doesn't interfere with my sleep, I don't care what you do with those damn things."

"All right then. See you in the morning."

The next day, sometime between breakfast and noon, George wandered into Ramon's shop. He gawked in surprise when he found Clint sitting at one of Ramon's tables with several bits of metal spread out in front of him. "What the hell are you doing here?" George asked.

"I own this place," Ramon grunted.

"Not you," George said as he pointed at Clint's table. "Him."

Clint looked up from what he was doing. He had a small section of a Winchester's firing mechanism in one hand and a magnifying glass in the other. "I told you I'd see you in the morning, didn't I? You're the one that's strolling in here so late."

"I said I'd see you in the morning, but I didn't think I really would. It was just one of those things you say. You know . . . like when you ask someone how they're doing? You don't really want to know and don't really expect an honest answer."

"Hmm," Clint said as he turned back to his table. "That's real fascinating. So when did you plan on heading back into those hills?"

"I thought we could head back there tomorrow, but if you're anxious to get moving . . ."

"I am. I'd like to see if there's anything left in the rest of those caves."

"So you believe I can find them?" George asked.

"I believe there's more to be found. As for the rest," Clint added with a shrug, "that remains to be seen."

George then turned his sights to Ramon. "What about you?" he asked. "Have you been as busy as my partner over there?"

"I looked through those boxes you dropped off if that's what you mean," Ramon replied. "Here's a receipt and my offer for payment."

Taking the slip of paper from Ramon, George shook his head and licked his lips like any other hungry scavenger looking down at a fresh kill. "I'm going to have to demand a better deal here. Considering how much I've brought you and how much is to come, I'm sure you can give me a better reason to keep my business here."

There was plainly some haggling that needed to be done and Clint didn't want any part of it. One advantage to playing the role of hired hand was the luxury of stepping aside when such tedious tasks needed to be performed. Strangely enough, just by looking at George's and Ramon's faces, someone might think they were engaging in an exciting game of cards.

Clint had more than enough to occupy his mind. Mostly, he was concerned with the rifle he'd been dismantling when George had arrived. It was one of the guns from the cave, but not one that he'd previously examined. It hadn't taken long for him to determine that this rifle had been constructed in a fashion similar to the rest. It had been pieced together from other quality models and modified to similar specifications, just not by him. Like any craftsman who knew his trade, Clint could spot his own work as easily as if he'd signed it. What he saw in this rifle was an attempt to copy his work. It was a fairly good attempt, but a copy all the same.

"All right then," George said triumphantly. "Do we have a bargain?"

Ramon nodded and shook George's hand. "We have a bargain. If I hear you take any of this gold somewhere else . . ."

"Don't worry about that. I'm a man of my word. Come on, Clint. Let's get started. There's plenty of work to do."

Clint may not have heard the specifics of whatever deal had just been struck with Ramon, but he knew he was more than ready to get back out to find more pieces to the puzzle of what the hell had happened to his rifles.

TWENTY-THREE

George was so excited once he got a look at the now-familiar range of caves that he damn near jumped down from the wagon he'd rented so he could run the rest of the way there. Using the map in his possession, George managed to find two more spots where items were being stored. It was late afternoon when he emerged from the second of those caves wearing a broad grin beneath a thick layer of dirt caked on his face.

"Lookee here!" George said excitedly. "I found something!"

Clint stood guard outside the cave, watching for any hint that the raiders who'd attacked them before might return. Although he'd seen some movement in the distance, there was nothing to make him certain it was anything to worry about. Even so, he wasn't about to turn his back on another possible ambush. "What is it?" Clint asked.

In George's hands was a long wooden box with ropes on either end that were fashioned into handles. "Don't know yet, but it's heavy."

"Is there any more in there?"

"I think so."

"How far back?" Clint asked as he squinted into the shadows of a cave that was barely tall enough for a man to move while crouching inside. "The last one was a tunnel that was a good forty yards long that had you crawling on your belly like a snake."

"I did the crawling, thank you very much," George said while setting the box down.

"And you did it for two cases of ammunition."

"*Specially made* ammunition," George corrected. "You said as much yourself!"

"I remember, but that doesn't make it valuable."

George leered at the box as he got down on both knees so he could reach for the lid. His hands trembled slightly and his eyes widened as if he were about to peel the corset off of a woman. "That was one cave, but there are plenty of others. And this," he declared like a magician at the end of his trick, "is gonna be a good one!"

With that, George pulled off the top of the box with a grand sweeping gesture. Both men looked down to see what was inside, and when they looked up again, only one of them was smiling.

"Dynamite," Clint said. "I'll grant you, it's not exactly gold, but we can get a real bang out of it."

George slammed the lid down beside the box so he could dig beneath the sticks of explosives with both hands. "I don't know what you're so damn smug about. Both of us are either profiting or losing on this venture."

"We've attracted enough attention with that gold," Clint replied. "It's comforting to have a wagon full of things that won't draw so many men looking to shoot us."

"You've been worried about men coming to steal from us all day. So far, it's just us and the lizards out here."

"That doesn't mean we're safe. Could just be that the

men looking to help themselves to our gold are lazy and are waiting to take a run at us when we get back into town."

George dismissed that with a casual wave.

"Where's the next cave?" Clint asked.

Looking up from the box, George asked, "We can still sell this, right?"

"Sure. Won't bring you a fortune, but it should pay for some of our supplies."

"Maybe pay for the damn wagon I rented."

When George grabbed the box lid and brought it down swiftly, Clint stopped him by grabbing his wrist. "It may not be worth as much as you like," he said, "but it'll explode a lot worse than gold. Take it easy."

George nodded. "You're right. Sorry about that." He then put the lid gently back into place. "Perhaps I'm in a mood after crawling around in the dark all day. The cave where I found this box was slimy and foul."

"Probably an animal's den."

Looking down at his clothes and noticing the slick mess that was smeared all over him, he couldn't do much more than laugh. "Seeing as how we're partners in this venture, I don't suppose you'd want to explore the next cave or two on the list?"

"You brought me along to watch for robbers and guard the gold," Clint said. "I've already done more than my share of stumbling in the dark."

"Come on, Clint! At least take the next one."

At the start of this job, Clint would have been willing to do his share where the dirty work was concerned. Lately, however, the work had gotten much dirtier than expected. All he had to do was look at the putrid state of George's clothes for proof of that. Rather than mention that, however, Clint said, "I'm surprised you'd want to risk not being the one to open the next boxes we find."

"I'll roll those dice."

Clint shrugged and gazed out toward the seemingly endless row of caves. "I think about some of those first strikes we made, setting eyes on those stacks of crates, feeling the thump of my heart as they were pried open. Mmmm. That does sound a hell of a lot better than standing around out here in the sun."

"I know what you're doing," George grumbled while doing his best to brush off some of the mess.

"Doing?"

"You just don't want to get dirty."

"Since these caves we've found so far today have been disappointing, maybe the next one or two will be just what we've been waiting for. Fine. I'll do it."

When Clint started rolling up his sleeves, George responded by reaching into a pocket for his map. "The next one should be right over there somewhere," he said while pointing to a short row of caves that didn't look big enough to be used for a rat's nest.

"I imagine there's another good-sized space just inside that entrance," Clint mused. "Probably a nice tunnel as well so the valuables are kept well out of sight."

"I reckon so. You'll be needing the lantern, then."

"Hope you don't mind if I take a look inside whatever boxes I find while I'm in there. After all this time spent standing around looking at nothing but desert, I'm aching for something more enticing."

"I bet you are. Whatever you find, get a nice look," George said. "It'll do you some good."

Clint was about to try to tempt the other man again, but decided not to bother. George knew what was going on, and he was too tired to be swayed. Cursing under his breath, Clint had to admit defeat.

Now that he'd resigned himself to having to follow

through on what he'd been saying, Clint lost a good deal of his previous enthusiasm. "Fine. I'll have a look inside the next two caves, but that doesn't mean you just bask in the sun. Someone needs to watch for those gunmen."

"They won't return," George said. "After the beating we gave them last time, they're surely off somewhere far from here licking their wounds."

"If you believe that, then you're dumber than you look." Although his words had come out a bit harsher than he'd intended, Clint still meant every one of them. At the very least, they seemed to have the desired effect.

George lost his smugness and nodded. "All right," he said quietly. "I'll keep watch. Do you really think they'll come back?"

After a slight pause, Clint said, "Yes."

Now George didn't look so happy. "You do? How long do you think we have before we need to start worrying?"

Clint pointed down at the trails that would take them out of the rocky pass and back into the flatter portion of the desert. There were two paths that could be used by horses, and two men were riding up each of them on a direct route to the caves.

"I'd say we've got about another minute or two," Clint said.

TWENTY-FOUR

Although the caves were an inviting prospect in terms of seeking shelter, Clint didn't like the idea of backing himself into a spot that could be so easily blocked. So he climbed into his saddle and George got into the wagon's seat so he could move it up the pass. He made it less than fifty yards before pulling back hard on his reins.

"There's more of them coming up this side of the hill," George announced.

"That's right," one of the men on the lower path called out. "We've got men on either side of you."

"You already took a run at us," Clint said. "In case you need to be reminded, you lost."

"I'm not looking for a fight, Adams."

Clint squinted down at the four approaching riders. They'd come to a stop midway up the trail. Although the sun was glinting in his eyes and reflecting off the sandblasted surface of the exposed rocks, he recognized the man who was doing the talking.

"That's the one who led the gunmen who fired at us last time," George said.

"I know," Clint replied.

This time, the man stayed put just outside of pistol range. Clint reached for the boot of his saddle and removed the rifle kept there.

"You hear me, Adams?" the man shouted. "I said I don't want a fight with you."

"Too late," Clint replied. "You started it when you fired at me and my partner the last time."

"That was unfortunate."

"And here I thought you'd try to pass it off as a misunderstanding."

While the other three men around him shifted in their saddles, the man who spoke stood like a statue as he said, "There was no misunderstanding. You and that other fellow are helping yourselves to what doesn't belong to you and I aim to put a stop to it."

"You can't make a claim on anything we found!" George shouted. "After what you and your men did before, we're well within our rights to shoot you on sight."

"I know you better than that, Clint," the man shouted. "And you should know that you're in the wrong here. If you haven't realized that yet, I can explain it to you."

"You want to give an explanation?" Clint replied. "You can do it over a drink in a saloon. Surrounding me and my partner with a gang of armed men only tells me one thing and it's not that you're here to talk."

"I'm here for what's mine!"

"I already said what I'm going to say to you. We're moving along now. If you and your men don't let us go about our business, you'll get more fight than you can stomach."

George shifted uneasily in the wagon's seat, but held his ground.

At the bottom of the pass, the man let out a sharp, short whistle.

Turning toward the sound of movement, George stood up a bit in his seat to get a look at the portion of the trail that stretched up to higher ground. "Those men coming around the other side of the hill are closing in."

Clint rode up alongside the wagon and jumped down from his saddle. Hurrying to the back of the wagon, he reached for one of the closest boxes and opened it. "When I tell you to go, you go. Don't stop unless I give the order. Understand?"

"What have you got in mind?" George asked. "Are we making a stand?"

"I don't think we'll have to," Clint told him as he walked back to Eclipse and mounted the Darley Arabian. "Especially if we spend some of the gold we found today," he added with a wink while holding up the stick of dynamite he'd collected from the back.

George became even more uneasy when he saw Clint take a match from his pocket. Despite that, he gripped his reins and prepared himself to follow through on the orders he'd been given.

"Call your men off," Clint warned. "I'm only going to ask once."

Even though there was no way for anyone to miss those words as they echoed throughout the rocky pass, the men down below spoke quietly among themselves as if nothing had happened to disturb them.

"Suit yourself," Clint said. He then struck the match against the side of the wagon and touched the little flame to the fuse attached to the stick of dynamite. He waited for an inch or so of the fuse to burn away before tossing the dynamite in a high arc through the air.

The hissing fuse left a thin trail of smoke, tracing its path higher up the pass. Since Clint didn't have as good of a vantage point as George, he couldn't see the riders that were coming from that direction. He didn't have any trouble hearing them, however, as they discovered what had been sent their way.

"Holy shit!" one of the men shouted.

After that, all that could be heard was the clatter of shoed hooves against the rock followed by a clap of explosive thunder.

"Go," Clint said sharply.

George wasn't about to argue. He snapped his reins to get the small team moving up the trail.

The men at the bottom of the pass were no longer having their hushed conversation. All of them were staring up at the caves with guns in their hands. Clint tossed them an easy wave.

George was just about to disappear behind one of the large rock faces that made up the cave-infested ridge when Clint caught up to him. "Keep going," he said.

Nodding fiercely, George replied, "I wasn't about to stop. It's all I can do to keep these horses from bolting in opposite directions after that damned blast."

Clint snapped his reins and held on tight. Eclipse had been around plenty of gunfire and even a good amount of explosions, but the stallion wasn't exactly fond of those things. Since none of the men at the bottom of the pass were inclined to fire up at him, Clint dropped his rifle back into the boot so he could draw his Colt. All the while, his eyes searched for anyone looking to take a shot at him or get the drop on the wagon from any angle. So far, all he saw of those men were the dust trails their retreating horses had left behind.

George said, "Looks like they're not about to come after us. You think we can pick a few of them off from here?"

"Since when did you become so bloodthirsty?" Clint asked.

"Since I found myself in the same men's sights twice in a row. I'd rather be on the right side of the rifle barrel instead of looking down the wrong end again."

"We're not picking anyone off," Clint told him. "We're heading back to town."

George's voice was already losing its bluster as he shifted back and forth to survey the terrain on either side of the wagon. "But we've got miles of desert to cover between here and town. That leaves a whole lot of opportunities for another ambush."

"They won't ambush us again. Not just yet anyway."

"And how can you be so sure?"

"Because," Clint replied, "they want something. If it was something they could just take from us, at least one of us would be dead already."

George swallowed hard to get rid of the lump that had suddenly appeared in his throat. "You think they're after more than just the gold we found?"

"Yeah, but I'm not exactly sure what just yet."

Looking over at Clint while bringing his team back under control, George said, "There's something you're not telling me."

Clint's eyes were fixed on a point far beyond the trail in front of him. "That man who showed up today and the last time we were ambushed . . ."

"You mean the one who did all the talking?"

"Yeah. I've been doing some thinking and I finally figured out why he looked familiar."

"Really?" George said hopefully. "You know him?"

"He's Allan Preston, and judging by the state of those rifles we found, he's been through a whole lot of hell getting here."

TWENTY-FIVE

They got back to town without anyone shooting at them. Even so, it was one of the longest rides Clint had experienced in quite a while because he never stopped searching for a hint of where the next attack might come from. His eyes darted toward every rustling branch. His muscles were tensed in preparation of drawing his pistol, snapping his reins, or leaping from his saddle altogether. Nothing came, however, which shredded his nerves worse than broken glass being dragged over expensive silk.

Since there was no gold in the wagon that day, they rode straight to the livery and unloaded their haul on the spot. Once the boxes were all spread out on the floor, George went through each of them while Clint kept watch.

Trujillo was never a bustling place, which made Clint's job easier. If anyone came down the street in front of the livery, there was no chance Clint would miss it. For anyone to sneak up close enough to be a threat, Clint would either have to be blind and deaf or asleep. Even if someone tried to get to a rooftop or look through the window of a nearby building, they would have to either show themselves on the town's flat skyline or open a shutter.

Clint leaned with his back against the livery beside its front door. He wasn't the only person in the vicinity. A few locals sat on their porches, and every so often children would scurry by. All of them were part of the town, however, and Clint figured they could only help him in his task. That notion was proven when a couple of old men sitting in front of a general store stared down the street and started chattering to each other.

The children running in that direction stopped and scattered.

A few dogs barked.

Clint smirked at how his hunch had paid off. By the time he saw the two strangers round the corner and walk toward the livery, he'd had more than enough time to prepare himself for whatever was on its way. And yet somehow he was still surprised when he saw who'd broken Trujillo's natural calm.

The years had been kind to Felicia Stone. Her thick black hair was a bit longer and her movements were more guarded but she was every bit as beautiful as he'd remembered. As she got closer to him, Clint picked out a few beautiful parts of her that he'd almost forgotten about. Almost, but not quite.

Clint didn't recognize the man walking at Felicia's side, but it was obvious he was hired to keep an eye on her. His hand never strayed far from the gun holstered at his side, and his eyes locked on to Clint as if he was already thinking of ways to tear him apart.

In stark contrast to her protector, Felicia brightened considerably as she drew closer to the livery. Extending one hand to block the gunman's path, she said, "You can find somewhere else to go, Wes. I'll be fine."

"I'm supposed to keep an eye on you," the gunman replied.

"I can keep an eye on myself," she told him. "I've been doing it for some time. There was a cantina back there. Why don't you get something to drink."

Wes stared holes through Clint while standing in the middle of the street. Even though there was nothing coming from any direction, he looked as if he wouldn't have budged if a stampede of buffalo had charged straight through town.

Clint stepped forward and opened his arms. "Hello, Felicia. I was just thinking about the last time we saw each other."

She stepped into his embrace, wrapped her arms around him, and leaned her head on his shoulder. "I think about those nights, too. Still makes me quiver."

"I'm guessing you're here with Allan Preston."

"You guessed right."

Doing his best to at least make it appear that he was immune to her charms, Clint asked, "What do you want?"

"I'd like to have a word with you. Can we go somewhere more private?"

"You can have all the words you want right here."

"If you're concerned about your friend," she said while nodding toward the livery, "don't be. I'm not here for the gold."

"What makes you think we found any gold?" Clint asked.

Felicia raised one eyebrow and looked at Clint with a disbelieving grin. "Come now. Don't treat me like a fool. I know what's buried in those caves."

Clint shrugged in a way that told her nothing. "You're telling me you're not here just to pay me a visit?"

She sighed and looked around at the locals, who barely

seemed to take a passing interest in them. "I want to talk, but not out in the middle of the street. Surely you'd like to know what's been going on around here."

"Once the shots were fired at me, I stopped wondering and started concerning myself with staying alive. I can figure out the rest once the smoke clears."

Tapping Clint on the chest while remaining close enough for the scent of her hair to reach his nose, Felicia said, "I imagine you're just angry about the misunderstanding between you and Allan."

"I understand just fine. He shot at me and I shot back."

"Fine," she huffed. "He was the one who misunderstood. You're right and he's wrong. Better?"

"A little."

"Then come along with me so we can have our talk."

Clint held on to her and said, "I've got a better idea. Meet me at the Tres Burros Saloon in an hour. If I see Allan or any of those others there, I'll start shooting and figure it's in self-defense. You understand me?"

She nodded. "I don't want any of them to be there either."

"That includes Wes. Is he a friend of yours?"

"No," she laughed. "He's a friend of Allan's. Don't worry, though. I've gotten real good at slipping away without any of them noticing."

"Fine. See you soon, then."

She placed a kiss on his lips and stepped back. "Thank you for trusting me, Clint."

"Don't disappoint me. It could turn out real bad for those involved. I've had my fill of men announcing themselves by firing at me."

"I don't blame you." With that, Felicia turned away from him and walked off.

Clint stayed put for another minute or two so he could

watch the street. When he stepped inside the livery, Clint found George standing right there with rifle in hand.

"You in trouble?" George whispered.

"Not as such, but thanks for being there for me."

"Actually, I was staying inside where it was safe."

"I know," Clint said with a grin as he stepped inside and shut the door behind him. "I was joking. What did you find in those boxes?"

"Just supplies, ammunition, the dynamite, of course."

"Of course. Nothing more interesting than that?"

"Not really," George replied. "Apart from this." He picked up the lid from one of the boxes and turned it over. Stamped onto the wooden slats was the same emblem that had been pressed into the gold coins they'd found. "I suppose it's just a brand."

Clint took a closer look at the lid. Apart from the emblem and the nails sticking through the wood that had connected it to the box itself, there wasn't anything else to see. "Yeah. It just marks this as belonging to the same man who owns that gold."

"You still think it's Preston?"

"Most definitely."

"If I may ask . . . who was that woman you were talking to?" George winced and added, "I'll admit, I did hear some of what you were saying while I was—"

"Hiding in the livery?"

"I was going to say covering you, but whatever. You know that woman? Who is she?"

"It's a long story."

"You've got an hour to tell it to me," George said.

"Fair enough. Why don't I do that while we break apart those boxes to see if there was anything we missed?"

TWENTY-SIX

When Clint walked into the Tres Burros Saloon, the only thing that was different than any other time he'd been there was the woman sitting at one of the tables at the far side of the main room. Felicia sat with a glass of wine, which she raised in a silent toast when she saw Clint step inside. He crossed the room and went to the bar.

"Hey, Danny," he said to the barkeep.

Having already picked up a mug from below the bar, Danny filled it from the keg and set it down in front of Clint. "You and George still crawling around them caves?"

"More or less."

"Find anything?"

"Just some tools, a few sticks of dynamite, and a whole lot of spiders."

"Heard about the dynamite," Danny said. "Or I should say I heard when some of it went off. You two still got all yer fingers and toes?"

"Last time I checked. Has anyone been asking around about me, George, or those caves?"

Danny didn't say anything at first, but he seemed a bit

readier to speak when he saw the silver dollars Clint slid across the bar toward him. "That partner of yours doesn't know how to keep quiet about much," he said.

"I already knew that," Clint replied.

"Some men have asked if I think you two really found anything or if George is just full of hot air."

"What did you tell them?"

"The truth," Danny said. "All I know for certain is that you and him keep riding out to the desert. Some others know about George renting a cart. Other than that . . ."

"Yeah?" When he saw Danny glance down at the bar, Clint placed another dollar in the same spot. Before Danny could claim it, Clint slapped his hand down on top of the money. "Tell me what you have to say. All of it."

"There was a fella came through here not long ago. Not this last time you and George went into the desert, but the time before that."

"You know every time someone rides out of town?"

Danny shrugged. "Trujillo is a small town. After all the talking George was doing, you two have become a topic of conversation."

Sighing, Clint fought back the impulse to march straight back to the livery and punch George in his big mouth. "Who was this fella you're talking about?" Clint asked.

"I don't know his name, but he's about your height. Long, dark hair. Kind of looks like death warmed over."

"He asked about me and George?"

"Not by name. He came along and heard folks talking about all the wild stories George had been spouting off about. That's when he came to me and asked about who was going after the gold. He wanted to know how many of you there were, what you'd found, that sort of thing."

"How much did you tell him?"

"Not much more than what George already did," Danny replied.

Unfortunately, that didn't make Clint feel much better.

"I didn't mention your name," Danny added. "I swear that much. George is one thing but you . . . I know you're not the sort of man I'd want to cross."

Glaring at the barkeep until he was certain Danny was speaking the truth, Clint said, "Smart decision. What about her?" he asked while nodding toward the table where Felicia sat.

"She's awfully pretty," Danny said.

"Do you know her?"

"No. First time I laid eyes on her was today when she came in and sat there. She's been sitting there ever since."

Clint didn't have any trouble believing that. Felicia already knew plenty about him, and there wasn't any reason to think a bartender could tell her any more.

"But she's not the woman you should be concerned about," Danny continued.

Shifting his focus back to Danny, Clint asked, "What do you mean?"

"There's another pretty lady who's usually around here that's turned up missing lately."

"Drina?"

Danny nodded, obviously pleased that he'd finally produced a nugget of information that Clint didn't already have. "You know that fella I told you about before? That one with the long hair and sour face?"

"Yeah."

"Well, I wasn't the only one he spoke to."

Clint wiped the smug look from Danny's face when he

reached across the bar to grab him by the collar and pull him partway over. Danny had a man there to cover him in case a rowdy drunk stepped out of line, and he stood up from where he was sitting in a corner of the saloon.

"I've already asked you about who came around looking for me," Clint snarled. "I even paid you to tell me what you knew in that regard. In fact, I paid you twice. I'm through being so civilized. Now it's time for you to tell me the rest."

When Danny motioned for his hired muscle to stay put, the man in the corner of the saloon was all too grateful to take his seat instead of challenging the Gunsmith.

"You're right, Clint," Danny said. "Truth be told, this last part slipped my mind until now. I'll be glad to tell you. I wouldn't want a friend to be caught unaware by some angry woman."

Clint didn't even realize he'd taken Danny off his feet until he let him go and the barkeep dropped back down to the floor behind the bar. While Danny regained his footing, Clint asked, "Drina was angry?"

Danny nodded while straightening the front of his shirt. Now that everyone was back in their proper places, the customers inside the saloon who'd turned to watch what Clint might do turned back around to their drinks. "The last time you were here," Danny said, "after you left, that is, she worked herself up into a fit that she didn't see any of that gold you and George found."

"Why would she think she'd be entitled to any of it?"

"You know how some women are. They let you up under their skirts and they figure you owe them something in return. Or sometimes they think they can talk a man out of anything they like, and if they find out they can't . . . well . . . they tend to get their pretty little noses bent out of shape. It's always the pretty ones, too," the barkeep added thoughtfully. "They're always the ones who act like the world owes 'em something."

Clint wasn't sure what aggravated him more: Drina's thinking she could help herself to his money, or his getting a lesson on women from the likes of Danny.

Feeling comfortable again now that he was the one doing the talking, Danny grabbed a rag and started wiping the top of the bar. "Of course, it didn't help that some of the folks hereabouts fanned the flames by agreeing with everything she said. That's something else that pretty ladies get used to."

Clint turned to look around at the other customers. Judging by the nervousness etched into some of their faces, it wasn't difficult to figure out which of them had been stoking Drina's fire.

"She stormed out of here and came back a little later," Danny said. "Her mood hadn't improved. A while after that, the fella I was telling you about came along."

"She heard you two talking?" Clint asked.

Whispering as if she was right there with them, Danny said, "She hears damn near everything around here."

"Do you know where she went?" Clint asked.

"Not really. I wasn't about to follow her."

"I think I have a good idea. What did she and that other fellow talk about?"

"Can't say for certain," Danny replied. "They went to a table and spoke real quiet. I can tell you one thing. She was in much better spirits after they were through. So . . . that's all I know, Clint. No hard feelings?"

"Keep your ears open for anything else that may be a help," he said. "There'll be more in it for you if you come up with something that proves useful."

"Sure thing." Nodding toward Felicia's table, the barkeep said, "You probably shouldn't keep that one waiting. You want a drink to steel yourself?"

"Couldn't hurt. I'll take a whiskey."

TWENTY-SEVEN

Clint approached Felicia's table, pulled out a chair, and sat down. The two of them looked at each other without a word as Clint tipped back his whiskey, drained it, and set the glass down. Finally, he broke the silence by saying, "Hello, Felicia. It's been a while."

"Yes it has, Clint. From what I hear, the years have been kind to you."

"Have you been keeping track of me?"

"Don't flatter yourself," she said with half a laugh. She sipped her wine and made a face. "I should have known better than to ask for wine in a town like this."

"And you really should have known better than to drink it."

"It's not so bad after a few sips. That's what I keep telling myself anyway."

"So," Clint said. "Other than sampling the local vintages, what brings you to Trujillo?"

"You know damn well what brings us here."

Clint sat back in his chair and drank his beer without saying a word. He wasn't about to give her an inch in the conversation. Now that he knew what he was dealing with, any bit of information he could get from her could prove to be more valuable than the gold they'd pulled from the backs of all those caves.

Realizing what he was doing, Felicia sighed and said, "You're really going to make me say it."

"Yep."

"All right." She squared her shoulders and sat up straight as if she were a little girl preparing to address her class. "We're here to claim what was stored away in those caves."

"Which brings me to my first question," Clint replied. "Why couldn't you or Allan just get it yourselves?"

"Who says we couldn't?"

Clint smirked. "If you could have gotten it yourselves so easily, you wouldn't need to wait for me and George to find it first. For that matter, you wouldn't have needed the map at all."

"Could be there's only one map."

"See, that's the problem when you toy with someone instead of talking straight to them," Clint said. "One way may be cute coming from someone like you, but it shows weakness. The other would have told me you knew the answer one way or another."

Felicia's expression soured. When she took another sip of wine, it soured even more. "There's only one map. I knew I should have gone with my first instinct."

"Which was . . ."

"Which was to invite you to bed, ride you like a bronco, and talk to you afterwards. This conversation would have been much more pleasant that way."

"There's still time for that." Upon seeing the sly grin on her face, Clint added, "Later. Right now, let's talk business."

Felicia didn't even try to sway him with a frown. "Business," she said. "That is why I'm here."

"Why isn't Allan here with you?"

"Come now, Clint. After what's been going on lately, do you mean to tell me a meeting with him would be well received?"

"Good point."

"As for all of that shooting, I want you to know that I don't agree with any of that. I tried to tell him to approach you in a more civil manner, but with all that's happening, he hasn't been in much of a mood for talking."

"What's been happening?" Clint asked.

"A falling-out between Allan and his uncle."

"Jeb—" Before saying the name out loud, Clint lowered his voice to keep from drawing any attention his way. "Jebediah Preston?"

"That's right. Actually, it started out as a falling-out between them, and it's since turned into something closer to a war. Jeb and his kin owned a sizable piece of land in Texas, but a good deal of it was annexed by the Federals or the railroads or . . . I don't know which."

"Could be both," Clint said. "And it could be other ranchers as well. I was there a few years ago and saw how much the Prestons controlled."

"That was only one ranch."

"Which was as big as a town."

"That's right," she said. "Allan thinks that if they'd stuck to ranching and owning property, there wouldn't have been a problem. But Jeb wanted more. He wanted a cut from merchants and anyone else who set up shop on his land. He even set up his own men to keep the peace."

"I imagine his problems got worse from there."

"You'd be right about that. Allan confronted his uncle to try and get him to negotiate a deal with . . . whoever was after their land. Jeb's answer was to tighten his grip even further, which only made things worse."

"You've got to know who is trying to get that land," Clint pointed out.

"Allan won't tell me," she replied with no small amount of aggravation. "He says it's family business."

Actually, that made plenty of sense to Clint. It didn't seem to set well with Felicia, however, so he decided not to mention that to her.

"Jeb and his uncle were making one last effort to work something out," she continued, "when some more of the property was taken away. That was the last straw as far as Jeb was concerned, and he decided to tighten his grip on what he had left. There was a shooting near San Antonio and then . . ."

"Wait," Clint said sharply. "Back up. What shooting?"

"There were some horses stolen and some of Jeb's boys tracked down the thieves. A lawman and his posse from a town on some of the annexed property were already hunting them down and everyone collided in a gulley somewhere. There were words exchanged, nobody would budge in deciding who got claim to the robbers or the horses, then someone fired a shot and it all went to hell from there."

Although Clint was getting a vague idea of what had happened, he was also becoming aware of how much information Felicia hadn't been given. Some of the details weren't as important as others, but he had no way of knowing which details could make a world of difference.

Felicia must have seen some of the frustration on Clint's face because she said, "This is why I wanted Allan to speak to you directly."

"Let's just cut through the fat and get to what you know for certain. How does any of this link up to those caves?"

Happy to return to more familiar ground, Felicia told

him, "Jeb stashed money in places like that all across Texas."

"Makes sense that a man like him doesn't exactly believe in trusting his money to a bank."

"Exactly. He always told his family that if things got bad, they could head to any of those spots, regroup, rearm, and ride again. Allan told that very thing to me several times. Regroup, rearm, and ride. After Jeb's men locked horns with the law that first time, things got real bad. At one point, his kin and anyone close to them were rounded up and scattered in all directions. I was in a small group that was brought south into Old Mexico.

"There were half a dozen men escorting me, a few other women, and some children. By the time we got away from those that were hunting us down, all but one of the men were killed. We even lost two of the women and a little boy named . . ." Tears started to form in her eyes, which Felicia quickly swiped away. "It was terrible," she said in an unsteady voice. "We couldn't fight anymore, so we divvied up what we had and we stored it away."

She sipped her wine, and Clint gave her a moment to compose herself.

TWENTY-EIGHT

"You helped stash it?" Clint asked after a moment.

"Yes, but I only had a few coins and some blankets."

"What's the story with those coins? It must have been a lot more trouble to melt gold down and cast them into those things than to just keep it in nuggets or bars."

Felicia let out a slow breath. "Jeb's crazy," she said. "That's the story. I always thought he was, but since things took a turn for the worse, he's gotten worse as well. It used to be that he was just another rich Texan with a whole lot of land. Now he thinks he's the lord of his own country. He's the law, he makes the rules, he thinks the currency should have his design. Like all of that makes it official somehow."

"I'd heard something along those lines," Clint mused. "It's just hard to believe."

"Well, believe it. Jeb and his men have squirreled away plenty more throughout these parts. Somehow Allan caught wind of what was up here. I guess those folks in that group I was in already knew of a few hiding spots because we sure weren't carrying enough to bring on all of this fuss."

"The Preston clan must be pretty big to start something as widespread as all of this."

"Between the family, the workers, and the hired guns, there's enough to make plenty of noise," she said. "This whole feud started right around the time when you left a few years ago, and both sides have added to their ranks. Gunmen and killers were hired on and paid in gold. After that, more of that filth came swarming in to claim their share."

"Another good reason for that gold to be marked," Clint said. "Better than posting an advertisement in a few newspapers."

"Good God," Felicia said as she took another long drink from her wine. "If I'd known how this would have ended up, I never would have associated with anyone named Preston."

"How were you drawn into this family?" Clint asked.

She blinked a few times and squinted as though his face had suddenly become covered in fog. "What?"

"I was told you're Martin Stone's granddaughter . . ."

Shaking her head, Felicia told him, "Jeb is my grandfather."

Now it was Clint's turn to seem confused.

"My last name has always been Preston," she explained. "When certain members of the family started staking their claim and trading shots with the locals, we took a different name to have some measure of peace. Stone is just the last part of Preston. Not much of a stretch, really."

Clint leaned back. "So that makes things different."

"Not really. Our family has never seen eye to eye with one another. Parts of it break off from the rest, they never speak again, and when they come back, it's like they're from opposite sides of the world. My part of the family came back just to live off a plot of Texas land to do some farming. Maybe raise a few head of cattle. Now . . . there's this calamity."

"This feud may be convoluted, but it doesn't sound so bad," Clint told her.

"It doesn't? Are you sure you heard everything I just told you?"

Reaching across the table, he placed a hand upon hers and looked her straight in the eyes. "It sounds like a terrible situation that's gotten way out of hand, but it all boils down to one simple thing. A man wants more power than he can rightfully grab. Fact is, that's what most blood feuds boil down to."

"Somehow that doesn't seem to help matters very much."

"Maybe not, but it helps to look at something's essence." Clint took a moment to think and then nodded as he reached his conclusion. "I need to have a word with Allan. He's your . . . what? Cousin? Doesn't matter. I want to talk with him."

"Just so long as you promise not to shoot him."

"I'm not the one that fired the first shots," Clint reminded her. "His men, on the other hand . . . they're a different story. If I'm to talk with Allan, it'll have to be just me and him."

"Actually, he mentioned something along those lines as well. About speaking with just you, I mean."

"See? There's hope for . . ." Clint felt optimistic for all of two seconds before it passed. The way Felicia was looking at him didn't leave much room for anything resembling hope. "What?" he asked. "What's wrong? You look like you just swallowed a worm."

"What I just said . . . it wasn't exactly true." Squirming in her seat, she looked at Clint with a hopeful smile.

He didn't return it. If he wasn't allowed any hope, she damn well wasn't getting any for herself.

Reluctantly, Felicia continued, "He said he wanted to speak with your partner. You know . . . George Oswalt?"

"Yes," Clint growled. "I know George Oswalt. He can speak to me instead."

"Allan . . . he thinks . . . well . . ."

"Just spit it out, for Christ's sake."

"He thinks you're just a gunman," Felicia said. "He wants to speak to the boss of your outfit."

"It's just me and George," Clint said. "That's hardly an outfit."

"He told me it would be a smart decision to kill you. The only reason he let me come to see you like this is because I doubt Allan would mind if I came back or not."

"Damn. That really is some family you got there."

"See why I don't want to associate with them?" Felicia said.

"Do you at least know what Allan wants with what's stashed in those caves?"

"That's the largest deposit the Prestons have in Old Mexico. It goes on for miles."

"Miles?"

She nodded and leaned forward to speak in a fiercely guarded tone. "It was charted on several different maps and Allan only has part of one. Jeb's got the others, but they're not as valuable as the one that got away from him. Allan says there's enough in there to turn the tide of this fight before it gets out of hand."

"*Gets* out of hand?" Clint chuckled. "You mean it's not there already?"

Felicia didn't find that the least bit funny. "Jeb's drawn enough of the wrong kind of attention already. Between the Federals and the law, he's got men in badges coming round every day. Then the gunmen started coming. Lord only knows who hired them, but killers were looking to clean the Prestons out of Texas before me and Allan and the rest decided to pick up stakes and leave. It only gets worse from there."

"Yeah. You're right about that. Just see what you can do about getting me that meeting with Allan."

"And if he'll only talk to your partner?"

"You're a persuasive woman. You'll come up with something."

TWENTY-NINE

When Clint left the saloon, he took a few steps out the door, found a spot where he could put his back to a wall, and took a good look at the street. As usual, there weren't many people to be found in the immediate area, and the ones he did see weren't in much of a hurry. They all looked like locals as far as he could tell. At the very least, none of them stood out as gunhands from Texas.

He didn't have to wait long before Felicia stepped outside as well. She stepped up to him and asked, "Will I see you later?"

"You mean for another meeting?"

"Of a sort. I'd prefer less talking, though."

"Sounds good to me."

That was enough to put a smile on her face and a spring in her step as she walked away. Clint allowed himself to watch her for a few seconds but then he took another gander at the street.

The same locals were there, doing the same things they were before. If anyone was keeping an eye on Felicia from a distance, they were doing it from too far for Clint to worry about. Just to be on the safe side, he started walking in the opposite direction he truly wanted to go.

Trujillo was a small enough town that he could have walked around the entire place in little to no time at all. He wasn't about to take an easy route, however, and he wove through the little Mexican settlement like a drunk trying to find his way home. After taking that overly long walk while checking behind him and all around, he was convinced that nobody was watching him either.

Clint still took a roundabout way, but eventually arrived at Ramon's shop. Fortunately, Ramon himself was never far away from his money and other people's gold. After walking up the creaking stairs attached to the back of the building, Clint knocked on the door.

There was no answer, so he knocked again. He was about to give up when the door was jerked open so quickly that it nearly made him jump out of his boots.

"Christ!" Clint said. "I didn't even hear a board creak."

"It's my place," Ramon said from behind a sawed-off shotgun. "I don't have to creak a damn thing if I don't want to. What the hell do you want?"

"Has anyone come around asking for anything out of the ordinary?"

"You mean like Preston gold or train robbers?"

"Train robbers?"

"That's right," Ramon said as he scowled at Clint over the top of his shotgun. "If you ask me, that is a much better explanation for someone trading so much gold."

"So that's why you haven't lowered your gun?" Clint asked. "You think I'm a train robber?"

"That's what those marshals told me."

"Did these marshals show you any badges?"

Clint got his answer through the uncertain look in Ramon's eyes and the slight waver in the hands wrapped around the shotgun. Holding both hands out to show they were empty, Clint said, "I just came by to ask if anyone's been sniffing around about me and I think I got my answer."

"They're not marshals?"

"You deal in healthy amounts of money and the sort of men that come attached to it. You must have a nose for who's lying about it and who's just trying to get their hands on more of it."

Ramon lowered the shotgun so the barrel was no longer aimed at a spot between Clint's eyes but still poised to do some damage if his finger twitched. "Who's supposed to be asking around about you?"

"He's about my height," Clint told him. "Long, dark hair. Sunken features."

"Name?"

"Allan," Clint replied. On a hunch, he decided to gamble. "Allan Stone."

The shotgun was lowered a bit more. "That ain't his real name, is it?"

"It's close, but no. That's not his real name."

Finally, the shotgun dropped the rest of the way and Ramon stepped aside. "Come in," he said, "before anyone else gets it in their head that I'm open for business at such an hour."

Clint stepped inside. The room was the same size as the shop downstairs, which wasn't saying much. It felt cramped enough when he was bringing gold in to be assessed but even worse now that he was sharing such close quarters with a bed, a kitchen table, and too many bookshelves. Before shutting the door, Ramon stuck his head out and looked back and forth.

"Expecting someone else?" Clint asked.

"There's been too many sons of bitches circling my shop. And not just the usual kind who are looking to rid themselves of stolen property. They're a whole new breed attracted by the likes of you."

"Me?"

"Yes, you, damn it!" Ramon grunted as he slammed his door shut. "All that blasted talk of Preston gold and whatnot. It gets the wrong folks all riled up, and this part of Mexico is already bursting with the wrong folks."

Clint let out a tired laugh. "Hopefully you don't lump me in with that group."

Ramon laughed as well. It wasn't until then that he finally seemed to let down his guard to become the same man Clint had dealt with before. "I take it you know this Stone fellow. Apart from the fact that he's after you, that is."

"We've met before. He's posing as a marshal?"

"Not him," Ramon said. "It was one of the men with him. Mean-looking bastard. He didn't say much after clearing a path for Stone. They asked about the gold, but seemed more interested in who was bringing it in."

"Did you mention me or George?"

"Hell no!"

That surprised Clint. Even though he'd figured Ramon for a man with a backbone, he knew the Mexican didn't owe him any loyalty that could put him in harm's way.

"Don't get all sentimental about it," Ramon said after having picked up on something in Clint's expression. "A man in my line of work has got to protect his customers' privacy. Unless a customer is some no-good outlaw, which I don't think you are. If I posed a threat to my customers, that would be bad for business and bad for my health."

"That being said, however, more trustworthy customers might be worth a little extra service."

"How much service?"

"If you could point me in the right direction of these men, I'd be much obliged," Clint said.

After a short amount of consideration, Ramon said, "Doesn't seem like a stretch, especially since they were so keen on finding you in the first place. They're staying in a cabin outside of town. At least, that's where some of them can be found. I didn't pay them a visit myself, but I was told I can go there with information if I decided to get on their good side."

"Can you tell me exactly where this cabin is?"

"There are a lot of cabins out that way and they only told me a general direction, but I'm guessing that's so they could see me coming. Considering what part of town it's near, I can narrow it down to two places that aren't being used by someone else. If they decided to take over one of the occupied cabins . . ."

"I can risk it. Thanks, Ramon."

"One more thing . . ."

"Don't worry," Clint said quickly. "I'll make sure you're compensated for this help. If it pans out, I'll set aside some gold you can keep for yourself."

"That's not what I was going to say, although I will accept that offer. You should be aware that those men aren't your only concern."

"Oh?"

Ramon nodded. "Drina came by here and she was fit to be tied. She wanted to know all about what you and George found. I wasn't about to tell her much of anything, but she already seemed to know. When she didn't get much out of me, she dropped your name. When that didn't make any difference, she stomped out of here like she was on a crusade. I gotta tell you, a woman on a crusade is hardly ever a good thing."

Suddenly, a few more of the questions in Clint's mind

were being answered. He mulled them over and thought about the next few moves he wanted to make. "Thanks again, Ramon. I appreciate the help."

The merchant said nothing, but his eyes remained fixed on Clint. He waited until Clint had the door open and one foot outside before speaking up again. "Clint."

Clint stopped and turned around.

"You can keep that extra payment," Ramon said. "Just do me a favor and make sure those men don't come back around here to make good on their threats. I'm not a man who's easily scared, but it's only a fool who ignores someone that poses a real threat. Those men . . . they're killers. I could see it in their eyes."

"You're right about that, and I don't intend on letting them hurt anyone. Even so, it might be best for you to close up shop for a few days until this matter is straightened out. Is that gold in a safe place?"

Ramon nodded. "Safest place within a hundred miles."

"Good. Keep it there and watch your back."

"You do the same, Adams."

THIRTY

The one-room cabin was dark, despite the efforts of a sputtering candle melting into a saucer. Drina sat in a rocking chair, staring at the bag containing several days' worth of clothing and sundries. There were just enough furnishings for someone to live in the cabin for a short stay. A small bed sat in one corner, and the opposite side of the room contained a square table along with a potbellied stove. All of the windows were covered by filmy curtains. When a man walked past them outside, she could see his shadow rippling across the wrinkled fabric.

Drina reached into a pocket of her skirt for a Derringer pistol, which she clasped in one hand. The man outside walked straight to the back door, opened it, and entered the cabin.

"Who is it?" she asked as her grip tightened around the Derringer.

"Who else you expecting?" VanTreaton asked as he approached her. His tall frame seemed even more imposing beneath the cabin's low ceiling, and his skin seemed even darker in the shadows. He walked straight up to her and reached down to clamp his grip around Drina's wrist. Forcing her to reveal the Derringer, he looked into her eyes and asked, "Were you gonna use that on me?"

"N-No."

VanTreaton twisted her wrist until she let go of the pistol. "Damn right you weren't," he said while catching the little gun before it hit the floor. Regarding the Derringer as if it were a toy, VanTreaton tossed it aside. "What've you got for me?"

"Clint Adams," she said. "He's in town."

Suddenly, VanTreaton's hand gripped her throat. "I ain't paying you to tell me things I already know."

"He—he's already spoken to . . ."

"To who? Allan Preston?"

She tried to speak, but couldn't get the words out until VanTreaton loosened his grip. Finally, she told him, "No. Felicia Stone met with him. The other one . . . George Oswalt . . . hasn't turned up yet."

VanTreaton smiled. "Good. That means we've got some time to kill." He let go of her throat and held that same hand down to her. Drina took it and was helped up from the chair. "We paid you plenty. You'll need to prove you were worth it."

"I can probably think of a few ways." With that, she tugged on the edges of her blouse, which was already down far enough to expose her shoulders. She kept pulling while wriggling her upper body until the blouse came all the way down past her breasts.

He cupped her breasts in both hands and started to rub them. When she let out a little moan, he teased her nipples between his fingers. "You like that, don't you?"

"Yes," she whispered.

VanTreaton couldn't wait any longer. He ripped off her

clothes, tearing some of the material along the way. Although she flinched a few times at his rough, probing hands, Drina didn't shy away. In fact, she became more aggressive as well by stripping him from his clothing so she could take hold of his stiff cock in both hands.

"Sit down," she said.

Sliding his hands down along her sides, he said, "Yes, ma'am," before taking a seat in the rocker.

Drina grabbed the back of the chair and slid her legs beneath the high armrests so she could sit facing him on his lap. Reaching down, she guided him between her legs and took his rigid pole inside her. Between the motion of her body and the back-and-forth movement of the chair, she was soon riding him in long, even strokes.

He wrapped his arms around her and ran his hands along her back. When they came to a rest upon her hips, he leaned back as much as he could and let her grind up and down on his thick cock. Drina arched her back and pressed her tits against his face. He opened his mouth and began flicking his tongue on her erect nipples.

VanTreaton licked between her breasts, all the way along her neck, before grabbing the back of her head and kissing her full on the mouth. Their tongues slid against each other and they pumped their hips together in unison. When the chair rocked forward again, VanTreaton grabbed hold of her backside and lifted her in one smooth motion.

Drina hung on tight by wrapping her arms and legs around him. His cock was still inside her, and she could feel it move with every step. VanTreaton carried her to the table and set her down on the edge of the wooden surface. Spreading her legs wide, Drina rubbed his muscular arms and waited for him to commence. In a matter of seconds, he was pounding into her once again.

Holding her knees apart, VanTreaton looked down to watch his cock slide in and out of her pussy. He pumped harder until he thrust between her legs like a piston. As her body began to tremble, she moved her hand lower to rub his thick column of flesh as it moved in and out of her.

Her orgasm came swiftly and she dug her nails into VanTreaton's shoulders as it swept all the way from the spot where he impaled her to fill every inch of her body. She was still shaking when he turned her around to bend her over the table. Drina grabbed on and pressed herself against the table as VanTreaton settled in behind her. One of his hands rested upon her hip while the other was used to guide his penis between her thighs. Soon, she was filled by him again and she let out a breathy moan until she'd taken every inch of him inside her.

"Harder," she grunted. "Harder."

He smiled and eased back until he was almost out of her. Then, he drove into her with enough force to shake the table upon its legs.

"Yes!" she wailed.

VanTreaton kept one hand on her shoulder and placed the other on her hip so he could feel her body tremble as he pounded into her. Drina's pussy gripped him tightly and her entire body clenched with another climax but VanTreaton wasn't about to let up. He drove into her in a solid rhythm, burying his cock between her legs while grunting in satisfaction. Soon, he gripped her ass in both hands and pumped one last time before exploding inside her. After he was spent, he gave her rump a few quick pats and stepped away from the table.

Drina turned around and sat on the edge of the table. One hand wandered between her legs to brush her fingers through the damp thatch of hair between them. "Where are the others?" she asked.

"Others?" VanTreaton asked as he picked up his pants and started pulling them on. "You only have to keep me happy, if that's what you're worried about."

"No. I mean the others that came with you. What if they come in here?"

"Then they'll get an eyeful. What do you care anyway?"

"I don't. Not really."

Buckling his gun belt around his waist, VanTreaton studied her carefully. Even in the dim light coming from the nearby candle, he seemed to be able to look straight through her. "You seem nervous. What's wrong?"

"Why does anything have to be wrong?"

"After what we just did," he said, "we should both be feeling mighty good. Instead you look like you're about ready to crawl out of your skin."

"You took me by surprise," Drina said. "That's all." She then walked across the cabin to the stove, where a small box of supplies was kept. "I've got a little food. Why don't I fix us something to eat?"

After watching her for a second, VanTreaton scowled and turned his attention back to finding the rest of his clothes. "Nah. I've got things to do. I'll let Cal know you're tucked away nice and safe. You should be ready to move. We might be riding out of here at a moment's notice."

"Don't go," she said quickly.

"What the hell's wrong with you? First you seem nervous that I'm here and then you don't want me to leave."

Drina had been watching him while trying to keep a smile on her face, but her eyes darted over to the window close to the front door. Then she looked at the door itself as it was opened.

Clint stepped inside as if he were strolling into his childhood home. When VanTreaton started to reach for his gun, Clint drew his Colt in one fluid motion.

"Don't embarrass yourself in front of the lady," Clint said. "Drop the gun belt before I put you down like a rabid dog."

THIRTY-ONE

"I'm sorry, John," Drina said to VanTreaton. "I didn't have a choice. He found me before you got here."

"Shut yer damn mouth, bitch," VanTreaton snarled. "I'll take care of you later."

"No, you won't," Clint told him. "And unless you play your cards right, you won't be doing anything to anyone else again."

Turning his angry gaze toward Clint, VanTreaton grunted, "What do you want?"

"I want to know where your partners are."

"I tried to find that out for you, Clint," Drina said. "Honestly! I asked him about them so you wouldn't have to go through the trouble."

"Keep quiet," Clint snapped.

"But . . ."

"You meant to stab me in the back by throwing in with this jasper and his friends," Clint said. "Just because it didn't work out for you doesn't mean I should be grateful to you for anything."

Drina opened her mouth but choked back any words

she might have been about to say. Then, she pressed a hand to her mouth as if to prevent anything from slipping out.

"Good," Clint said after Drina proved she could keep quiet. "Now get over into that chair and stay there."

She found a chair in a corner, wrapped herself in the dress she'd stripped out of not too long ago, and sat down.

"As for you," Clint said to VanTreaton. "Go ahead and strap that gun belt on."

"What?"

"You heard me. Go ahead and arm yourself. Otherwise, you'll just be preoccupied with trying to get to your gun and you won't listen to what I have to say. I don't like repeating myself, so let's just get this part over with."

VanTreaton kept his eyes on Clint as he squatted down and felt around on the floor with one hand. His fingertips brushed against the leather of the gun belt he'd dropped, but he eventually had to glance down to make sure he was grabbing it properly. When he looked back to Clint, he was even more tightly wound than before.

Clint waited until the gun belt was buckled around VanTreaton's waist before speaking again. "There. Now that that's out of the way, are you ready to pay attention?"

VanTreaton watched Clint closely. His hand drifted toward the pistol holstered at his side, and his eyes took on a steely glare.

"Or would you rather be stupid?" Clint asked. "If that's the case, then I'd rather you go ahead and get it out of the way to save us both a lot of time."

"You think I won't do it?" VanTreaton growled.

"I'm not quite sure, to be honest."

"You made a mistake letting me arm myself."

"You think so? I guess we'll find out. The way I see it, there's only three choices. You can draw first, kill me, and celebrate with the lady over there. I can draw first, kill you, and go about my business."

After waiting for a second of intolerable silence, VanTreaton asked, "The third?"

"We can have the talk I came here for and then both be on our way. You make the call."

Sizing up the man in front of him, VanTreaton eased his hand away from his holster.

"Good decision," Clint said. "You're here on Preston's behalf, but not Allan's."

VanTreaton's eyes narrowed as he turned a hateful stare toward Drina's corner.

"I had to tell him!" she cried. "He showed up before you arrived and he forced me!"

Actually, when Clint had found the cabin where Drina was staying, she'd let him inside willingly. Their conversation had been relatively short and she'd parted with what little she knew relatively easily. A guilty conscience tended to do that to some folks, especially when they figured there was no way of coming up with a lie good enough to get them out of their predicament.

"Shut yer damn mouth," VanTreaton said to her.

"Don't be too cross with her," Clint said. "I would have figured it out. Every time I've seen Allan Preston, he's had a small group of men with him and you've never been one of them. Since every member of the Preston family is after this gold, it stands to reason that *El General* would send some men of his own down here to fetch it for him. What really tipped the scales is that you never asked her about the map. Isn't that what you told me, Drina?"

She turned away from them both. Like most backstabbers, she preferred to be long gone before having to answer for whatever she'd done.

"Yeah, I work for Jeb Preston," VanTreaton said. "That ain't no secret. Just like it's no secret that he knows where his own damn gold is hid."

"Which brings me back to my first question. Where are the rest of Jeb's men?"

"They're here," VanTreaton said with a cruel grin. "Here and there. Waiting."

"Waiting for what?"

"Waiting for someone to slip up, and they didn't have to wait long, now did they?"

Clint was starting to get lost, but figured all he needed to do was keep the man talking. Eventually, he would say everything Clint needed to hear. "You're talking about how Allan slipped up?" Clint asked, even though he had no idea if Allan had slipped up about anything at all.

Clint's poker face must have held because VanTreaton nodded right away. "Yer damn right he slipped up! Breaking away from the Corps is something only a fool would do, especially since Jeb's got close to an entire county locked up with more to come. For a Preston to break away . . . well that's a goddamn mortal sin."

"The core?" Clint asked.

"No. The Corps. A group of men, training and working together." VanTreaton's face cracked apart into a smug grin. "When you were at the ranch them years ago, Jeb was a businessman looking out for his interests."

"He was forming a militia," Clint said.

"Call it what you like, but he did more than that. He put together the Corps, and a good part of that was on account of them Clint Adams Specials you made for him. I wouldn't have thought so much could be accomplished with a batch of rifles, but I'll be damned if I wasn't wrong."

He was very wrong about that, Clint knew. For proof, all anyone needed to do was look at how things were before and after the contributions of men with names like Colt and Winchester. But Clint wasn't about to mention any of that. VanTreaton was pleased with himself enough already.

"Them guns you made," VanTreaton continued. "They were real quality merchandise. When Jebediah put them in the right hands, things really started swinging his direction. The raiding parties he sent out were like demons. They'd clean out anyone who stood in their way."

"There's more to it than that," Clint said.

"Sure there is. Jebediah Preston is a great man."

"Sounds to me like he's a ruthless killer in charge of other ruthless killers."

"Call 'em what you like. They got the job done."

"But that great man of yours couldn't even keep his own family together," Clint said. "Doesn't sound so impressive to me."

"Ain't nobody's perfect."

"Tell me where the others are."

"Go to hell," VanTreaton snapped.

Clint looked over to Drina. "Then you'll tell me."

"I . . . I can't," she sputtered.

She was frightened for her life, but she knew. Clint was certain of that now. It was the look in her eyes and the tremor in her voice which told him even more than the fact that she'd said, "I can't," instead of, "I don't know."

"Yes you can," Clint said. "And you will."

"Please," she whined.

Suddenly, VanTreaton turned on her like an animal. "Shut yer goddamn mouth, bitch!"

"You're not leaving here with that gold," Clint said. "Jebediah Preston sent you here to do his dirty work because he's too yellow to do it himself."

"That's not true! He'll put you down yourself when he gets here."

"He's a coward."

"And you're a fucking ungrateful son of a bitch for not joining up with the Corps when you had yer chance!" VanTreaton roared.

"I know a losing hand when I see it," Clint told him. "And I'm looking at one right now."

VanTreaton spat out a string of obscenities that was nearly unintelligible as he reached for the gun at his side. The barrel of his pistol was about to clear leather when Clint drew his Colt and used it to drill two fresh holes through VanTreaton's heart.

VanTreaton twisted around on the balls of his feet, rolling with the momentum of the impacts, before dropping to the floor. He would take his angry, vaguely surprised expression to his grave.

THIRTY-TWO

"All right," Clint said as he walked over to VanTreaton's body. "You don't have to be frightened anymore." When he didn't hear a response, he looked up and over to Drina in her corner. "Did you hear me?"

"Oh . . . yes," she whispered as she pressed herself against the closest wall. "I thought . . ."

"Thought I was talking to him? He can't trouble you any longer. Can't do anything else to you either."

"He and I . . . it wasn't like with me and you, Clint."

Shaking his head, Clint picked up VanTreaton's gun and walked over to her. "No need for any of that. Just tell me what I want to know."

"But . . . I told you when you came over before—"

"You told me plenty of things," Clint interrupted. "Some of them I believe and some were boldfaced lies."

Peeling herself away from the wall, Drina stepped forward while trembling like a dry leaf on a bare twig. "Please don't kill me," she said.

"The only time you'd need to worry about that would be if you made a move as stupid as he did," Clint replied while nodding toward VanTreaton. "Fight back the urge to shoot me and you'll be fine. I'd also appreciate it if you could tell me the rest of what I want to know."

"I kept him busy for a while like you asked, didn't I?"

"Yes, you did. You also told me there were men in town who answer only to Jebediah Preston. Where are they?"

For a moment, it seemed that she might stick to her guns by insisting she didn't know. Then Drina took a long look at the carcass on the floor and thought better of it. "They're camped in one of the caves about a quarter of a mile south of town."

"How many are there?"

"Four or five. That's all I saw when I was there. Well," she added, "one less now."

"How do you know them?"

"I was angry when I heard George talking about all the gold he'd found. I thought we were partners on that venture."

"You got the venture rolling," Clint said. "For that, you wanted a fee and you were paid. That was the end of our deal."

"Well, I should have been given a taste of what you found. After all, you wouldn't have—" She stopped when Clint raised a hand, and she flinched as if she expected that hand to swat her across the face.

Clint didn't like a woman thinking that of him, but he didn't have the time or inclination to coddle her. "What did that one offer you?" he asked while pointing over to VanTreaton.

"It wasn't him who spoke to me. It was Cal Landry. He's a sergeant in Jebediah's Corps. He offered me five hundred dollars' worth of those gold coins if I showed them how to clean out Allan and his men. A thousand if I also brought the map to him."

"How long have Landry and the others been here?"

"Maybe two weeks or so. They've been watching the town and waiting to see how much you and George would bring back from those caves."

"Then what?"

"Then," she said, "he means to take it. But he's not as interested in the gold so much as he is in the rifles you found."

"I'll just bet he is," Clint said with a laugh. "Nice try, but it doesn't take much to come up with that after what you heard me and VanTreaton talking about a few minutes ago."

"I'm not making it up," she insisted.

Clint studied her and couldn't find anything in her eyes or mannerism to make him think she was lying. She was too damn scared.

"All right, then," he said. "I'll trust you. Do one more thing for me and I'll see to it that you get that gold you were promised."

"What do you want me to do?"

"Keep them away from the livery down on Cruces Street. At least until this time tomorrow."

Drina nodded vigorously. "I can do that. Usually one of them comes along every morning. They'll want to know what happened with . . ." She trailed off when she glanced in the direction of the dead body. In a somber tone, she said, "I can do that."

"Good. Don't you double-cross me."

THIRTY-THREE

"She's gonna double-cross you," George sneered.

Clint stood near the window of a small room. "You think I don't know that?" Clint snapped.

"Then why did you trust her?"

"I didn't trust her."

"That's not what I gathered after what you told me."

Allowing the lace curtain to fall back into place over the window, Clint sat down on a chair that was just a bit too small to hold a grown man comfortably. "She's angry about missing out on the gold, but she's no idiot. She just saw a man killed and didn't have it in her to lie about that other group of men being in town."

"Oh, I'm not worried about those other men being in town. I mean, considering what we found in those caves and how many more there are left to explore, it only makes sense that someone else would come looking for them. I don't think they've been here as long as she says, though."

Having spotted a bit of movement on the street outside, Clint glanced through the window to find an old stoop-backed drunk staggering from one darkened doorway to another. Considering dawn was only a few hours away, that was about all he'd seen out there since he'd arrived to bring George up to snuff on what had happened recently. "Why don't you believe that part?" he asked.

"Because . . . wouldn't they have made a move against us by now?"

"Why would they? They're after the gold. Gold is heavy. If you were in their shoes, wouldn't you sit back while someone else did all the heavy lifting?"

George sat upright on the bed with his back against the headboard and his legs stretched in front of him. His feet still nearly came to the end of the mattress. "Yeah, I see what you mean," he grumbled. "Especially since so much of that dragging was through those caves. Those goddamn caves. I almost wish I never heard of them with all the trouble they are." Glancing around as if he was worried about upsetting the fates, he added, "Almost."

Despite everything that had been happening, Clint couldn't help but laugh at the sight of George trying to get comfortable. "How on earth did you settle on this place for us to stay?" he asked.

"Before you went traipsing off to do . . . whatever you've been doing . . . I distinctly recall you asking me to find a safe spot to hang our hats."

"I did."

"Well," George said while stretching out his arms to encompass the entire quaint little room. "Here you go. Feels mighty safe to me."

"It might feel a little better if it was big enough for us both to be in here without knocking something over every time we turn around."

"Would you rather stay in a saloon or the hotel, where anyone with half a brain would come looking for us?"

Instead of dignifying that with an answer, Clint merely grunted as he tried to find a way to sit on his chair without hurting himself.

"Didn't think so," George said. "This room was being rented for next to nothing while the kid who normally stays here is working on her aunt's chicken farm. The woman who owns this house won't tell a soul we're here, by the way. She and I got along like old friends."

"Splendid."

George crossed his legs and folded his arms over his chest, which still didn't make him look like he was at ease on that bed. "So who's this man you shot?"

"John VanTreaton. He's worked for Jeb Preston for some time."

"And you tried to have me believe you never heard of Jebediah Preston."

"When I was in Texas at that time, he was using the name 'Martin Stone.' Allan Preston was using his real name, but he wasn't . . . forget it. That was then and this is right now. Got it?"

George shrugged. "I wasn't arguing that point."

"Then why were we talking about it?" When George shrugged yet again, Clint fought the urge to shoot him. After he took a breath, he got a better grip on his temper. Shooting would have been a bit much. Pistol whipping, on the other hand, seemed about right.

"So what do we do now?" George asked.

"I was getting to that. After I saw Ramon, I went to pay a visit to Drina. I knew she wasn't telling me everything just yet, but I asked her to keep VanTreaton busy for a while so I could collect some things to barter."

Sighing, George asked, "How much of the gold did you take?"

"None. I collected the rifles we found."

"Oh? You think they came back just for the rifles? I'm sure you did a fine job on them, Clint, but . . ."

"I don't think this is all about the rifles," Clint said. "But they're obviously something the Prestons want. Otherwise they wouldn't have been squirreled away."

"I suppose."

"Think of them more as a token of goodwill. When we have a word with the Preston gunmen, the rifles will prove we truly do have the goods taken from those caves and are willing to trade them."

Suddenly, George seemed even less comfortable in the small bed. "Which Preston gunmen?"

"All of them. Come the morning, we'll have a word with them to see if we can't work something out."

George's face paled. "You want me to go, too?"

"Both of our necks are on the line."

"Why don't we just take what we've got and ride out of town? I'm more than willing to admit when enough's enough. After all, wouldn't want to be greedy."

Clint didn't try to hide the fact that he was enjoying the display George was putting on as he tried to salvage a bit of his dignity. "That sounds fine," Clint said. "Just as long as you think either of the two groups will just let us take their gold and be merrily on our way."

"*Their* gold? It was in the back of a cave, for Christ's sake."

"It has their brand stamped on it."

"Sure, but . . ." George tried to think of a reasonable reply to that and came up empty. "There's plenty more," he said quickly. "I'll even leave the map. I know! We can throw in the map as another bargaining chip!"

"Right!" Clint said. "I'm sure that'll be enough to keep

them happy. After all . . . they surely wouldn't want to get greedy."

For a brief moment, George tried to believe that Clint was being serious. When that passed, he rolled onto his side, nearly fell off the bed, and grunted, "I hate you."

THIRTY-FOUR

That night, Clint wound up sleeping very well. He slept better than George, which wasn't saying much since George alternated between sweating nervously about what the next day held for him and trying not to roll onto the floor.

Clint was in good spirits. Although there was still a good amount of work that needed to be done, he knew most of what lay in front of him and how he was going to deal with it. All that remained for him at the moment was to enjoy the breakfast of ham and eggs cooked for them by the woman who owned the house where they'd slept.

George, on the other hand, wasn't so optimistic. When he walked down the stairs and to the woman's kitchen, he could barely lift his boots. When he ate, he stared down at his meal as though it was the last one he would ever enjoy.

Knowing better than to try and cheer the other man up, Clint simply led him to the Tres Burros Saloon, where they'd arranged to meet with Felicia. Clint sat at the table where he'd met with her before and ordered coffee from Danny. George did the same.

"Maybe you should drink something with a little more kick," Clint said.

"It's a bit early for that, don't you think?"

"Normally, yes. Today, I think you could use something to loosen you up. You look like a watch that's about to pop a spring or two."

George sighed. "I'll be fine. Just give me a minute."

Standing up and removing his hat, Clint said, "You've got a few seconds. Here they come."

Following Clint's lead, George stood and politely nodded as Felicia approached the table. She wasn't alone and the tall man with the sunken features accompanying her seemed even less happy about being there than George did.

"Hello, Felicia," Clint said. "Allan."

Felicia smiled and sat down. Before she could return the greeting, Allan said, "We've wasted enough time already."

"Agreed."

"So let's get down to why we're here. I want the gold, the rifles, and anything else you may have found in those caves. I also want the map."

"Anything else I can offer you?" Clint asked.

"Don't be a smart ass, Adams. Those things are mine by right. More mine than yours anyway."

"What do you need them for?" When he saw Allan tense as though he was about to lunge across the table, Clint swiftly added, "The only reason I ask is because I've also met with John VanTreaton. You remember him, right?"

Through clenched teeth, Allan replied, "Of course I do."

"Seems to me that you men had a falling-out as of late."

"What's that to you?"

"Seeing as how we're the ones who have what you

want," Clint replied, "it seems pretty important to figure out who we're dealing with. You've got to know that VanTreaton and his boys want the same thing you do."

"Hardly," Allan said.

Felicia placed her hands flat on the table as if she were spreading out a contract in front of them. "Let's not get wrapped up in threats and whatever else you boys had in mind to see who's the bigger dog here. We all know what we're here for and what's at stake. Let's negotiate a way for all of us to leave happy."

Staring across the table at Allan, Clint said, "You had the chance to finish this a couple of times already. Those times when you had your men ambush us, you stayed back and barely lifted a finger to—"

"You should feel damn lucky I stayed back," Allan snapped. "Otherwise, you'd be dead."

"Why not finish the job?" Clint asked. "Or at least try to finish it?"

"Because I'm not a bloodthirsty animal like my uncle. He's out of control and running roughshod across southern Texas. I'd hoped he would come to his senses when the Federals and law came to pick away from his territory, but it only made him angrier. Our family stretches back farther than him, and I won't have everything we built up be lost in a senseless fight or pissed away on some foolish dream."

"How many men do you have on your side of this?" Clint asked.

"Doesn't matter," Allan told him.

"I beg to differ," George said. "If I'm to throw in with anyone, I need to know I'm signing up on the winning side."

Looking over at George as though he'd only just acknowledged the other man's existence, Allan asked, "Who the hell are you again?"

"I'm the one . . ." George paused so he could shoot a quick glance over to Clint. He then steeled himself and said, "I'm the one who knows where to find the other maps."

Suddenly Allan was very interested in what George had to say. "What other maps?" he asked.

When Clint saw that his partner needed a little prodding, he said, "Go on. Tell him."

THIRTY-FIVE

"I got this map because of a man who lives in a town on the border just on the Mexican side," George said. "He steered me to where I needed to go to get this map and told me there were others I could get later on."

"You didn't get them all at once?"

"It seemed this one would get me what I needed. Besides," George added, "there are always dangerous types who come along when the stakes get too high. The company at this table and elsewhere in this town is proof enough of that."

"So it is." Allan leaned back in his chair to digest what he'd heard. "What's this man's name?"

"We don't part with any information like that," Clint said before George had a chance to buckle. "Not until this matter is resolved."

Allan met Clint's gaze. "This is Preston family business. Not yours. What do you care whether it gets resolved or not?"

"Because people are dying and don't you dare try to tell me it's just Preston family members or even those hired by the family that are bleeding because of this idiotic feud of yours."

Neither Allan nor Felicia tried to say any such thing.

"Not only that, but several of those people were killed by my guns."

"Come now, Adams," Allan said with a cold smile. "You've made plenty of guns. Do you think all of them were used to shoot snakes or tin cans off of fence posts?"

"No, but I would never have taken the job if I'd known I was helping a madman stake his claim through fear and murder. Those rifles were supposed to be used by regulators on privately owned land. Not only that, but this feud has found its way back to me regardless. It ends here."

"Believe it or not," Felicia said, "but we're all of the same mind. We want this thing to come to an end as well. Too many of my family have died recently and my grandfather is to blame. We've tried working this out some other way, but he's too far gone for talking or negotiations."

"Maybe I should talk with him," Clint offered. "It's been a couple of years since the last time I met the old man, but we seemed to see eye to eye on more than a few things. Perhaps what he needs is to hear from someone outside of this mess."

"You're not exactly outside of it," Felicia said.

"It's either me or the law. I think he'd rather sit across from me."

"Too late for that," Allan said firmly. "Jebediah doesn't care what anyone outside of his family has to say. Lately, he barely cares what anyone inside of it has to say either. All he cares about is planting his flag anywhere he can, and he needs to collect his stockpiles to do that. VanTreaton and that animal Cal Landry have already buried plenty of men who thought they could get him to listen to reason. The standing orders are to gather those supplies and kill anyone who gets in their way."

"There's not much time left if we're to do anything

about this," Felicia said. "For now, Jeb's Corps is just seen as separate gangs of outlaws running through Texas and Mexico like so many other outlaws. Once Jeb's got his funding, he'll make himself known in a big way."

"He'll pay for men to rally around him," Allan said, "and shoot anyone who stands against him. It's insane for him to think he can succeed, but he'll sure as hell spill a lot of blood before it's over."

"VanTreaton is dead," Clint said.

The bluntness of that announcement caught Allan and Felicia off their guard. "You never mentioned that," Allan said.

Clint nodded and leaned forward so he could speak without being overheard. "That's because I wanted to make certain you were worthy of hearing the truth."

"What about Cal Landry?" Allan asked.

"I know where to find him and the men he brought along. Rounding them up should put a good-sized dent in Jebediah's plans. With enough persuasion, I'm thinking we should be able to arrange a meeting with the old man himself. No matter what, he's the key to all of this."

"We both agree on that," Felicia said. "One word from him, and the fighting is over. Without payment coming, those hired killers will crawl back inside whatever holes they came from. And without his blessing, the men who are truly loyal to him will stand down."

"If he won't end this willingly," Allan said, "we'll have to kill him."

"You'd do that to your own flesh and blood?" George said.

Without a flinch, Allan replied, "If it's got to be done, I'd rather be the one to do it. Me or someone within the family."

"That's all fine and good," Clint said, "but the old man's a bit out of our reach for the time being."

Allan grinned in a way that made him look like the face of death. "That's why we're bringing him here," he said.

"How could you manage something like that?" George asked.

Felicia drew a deep breath so she'd have the strength to say, "He's always had a weakness for his granddaughters. I sent word to him a few days ago that I was here and we made sure Cal and VanTreaton could confirm it."

"We also made it known that a good portion of his gold is in our hands," Allan explained. "Whether it's because of greed or whatever is left of his family honor, Jeb will be along soon. I'm guessing he's already on his way."

Clint pushed away from the table and stood up.

"Where are you going?" Allan asked.

"To confirm your story."

THIRTY-SIX

When Clint went to the livery down on Cruces Street, he didn't go alone. Not only was George with him, but Allan went along as well. Rather than waste time trying to talk Allan out of it, Clint settled for insisting that he remain out of sight while they went to check on the rifles they'd stashed. As soon as the livery was in sight, it was obvious that they weren't the only ones paying it a visit.

"That's Cal Landry's horse," Allan said when he spotted the dark gray mare tied near the trough in front of the livery.

"Looks like he's got some men with him," Clint said.

"Mangy dogs always travel in packs."

A few seconds later, George hurried toward them from the direction of the livery. He was out of breath and sweating when he said, "There's more of them behind the livery. I don't think any of them spotted me. I got close enough to count three of them."

"Stay here," Clint told him. "I'll go and have a word with them."

"If that's where you're keeping those rifles," Allan warned, "I doubt they'll be willing to speak to you."

Clint slapped his hand on the grip of his holstered Colt. "That's why I intend on doing my talking with this. Just stay out of sight." Without waiting for Allan to agree to those terms, Clint stepped into the street and hurried toward the livery. Just as he was spotted by a man stepping out of the livery, he shouted, "What the hell are you doing there?"

The man had just gotten outside and was carrying a bundle wrapped in a horse blanket. Keeping one arm wrapped around his cargo, he used his other hand to knock on the livery door behind him. Almost immediately, the door was opened by two more men. One of those was carrying a bundle similar to the one in the first man's possession. Clint recognized the other as Cal Landry.

Landry positioned himself in front of the livery's door. "We're reclaiming these rifles, Adams! If you know what's good for ya, you'll let us take the gold as well."

The bundles were the right shape for the rifles to be wrapped up in those blankets.

"You're not reclaiming anything, damn it!" Clint shouted.

"Go to hell, Landry, you son of a bitch!" Allan roared as he hurried over to stand at Clint's side.

"Wait!" was all Clint got out before guns were drawn and lead started to fly.

Landry cleared leather first and he pulled his trigger while sidestepping away from the street. His intent was obviously to provide cover so his partners could get away with their bundles. Allan stood his ground and returned fire, squeezing his trigger twice before the three men that George had spotted behind the livery came rushing around to join the fight. Allan was forced to find a spot that wasn't in the open.

"George, try to push them back," Clint shouted.

"What?" George cried. "Me?"

"Just point a gun at them and pull your damn trigger!"

George wasn't wearing just one pistol. He wasn't even wearing just two. He wore all three pistols he'd brought along with him when he'd made his first trek into the desert. Since he so rarely used the guns as anything more than decoration, even Clint had forgotten how many of them there were. When he tried to pick one to draw first, George wound up slapping at his shoulder holster and hip as if he were trying to smother flames that had spread to his clothing.

Rather than try to run for cover, Clint dropped to one knee so he could steady his aim. The livery was on the edge of pistol range, which meant it would take sheer luck or incredible skill for someone to hit him while firing so many rounds in such quick succession. By the time Clint had sent another round back at the livery, there was even more thunder exploding behind him.

Not only was Allan returning fire, but George had finally pulled the .44 from beneath his left arm and was blazing away. The next few seconds were filled with chaos and stank of burnt gunpowder. Gritty smoke hung in the air between the two groups of men, where it was churned by a slow Mexican breeze.

The first ones to escape from the confusion were the two men carrying the rifles away from the livery. Upon reaching the back corner of the structure, they hurried to the lot behind the place and disappeared from sight.

Cal Landry hunched over and made his way to an outhouse that was so old it practically leaned against the building next to the livery. Moments after he ducked behind the little shed, bullets impacted against the outhouse door to punch holes through the brittle wood while sending pops of dust into the air.

Since he no longer had a clear shot at Landry, Clint

shifted his aim toward one of the other gunmen. He squeezed off a shot that caused the younger man to curse and stagger to one side. The gunman managed to send one more wild shot through the air before he caught a series of rounds in the chest and arm. His body twitched from the impacts and the gun flew from his hand. He fell to the dirt and hit the ground with his chin, becoming deathly still.

One by one, Landry's men circled around the livery, where their horses were waiting.

"They're gonna get away!" Allan shouted. "Pour it on!"

George now had a pistol in each hand and was pulling his triggers as quickly as his fingers would allow. The more his guns bucked within his grasp, the tighter he clenched his eyes shut. Even so, he was at least keeping Landry and the gunmen by the livery too busy to take careful aim.

When Clint heard gunfire coming from yet another source, he turned around to get a look for himself. If they had been north of the border in Texas, he would have expected lawmen to have arrived. Instead, he saw a pair of men in long coats striding down Cruces Street. One of them fired a .45 caliber pistol while the other brought a scattergun to his shoulder and sent a load of buckshot at the livery. Neither one of them so much as flinched at the prospect of walking directly into the middle of a raging hailstorm.

There were no more targets in Clint's sight. The last place anyone had seen Landry was when he'd ducked behind the outhouse, so that's where everyone concentrated their fire. In a matter of seconds, the shabby little building was ripped apart. When the men in the coats got close enough, one of them nearly cut the outhouse in half with his scattergun. Now that there was a hole in the outhouse big enough for a dog to jump through, Clint could see there was nobody behind it.

"Enough!" Allan shouted. "They're gone."

"Yeah," George said with relief. "They're gone."

"They're not about to leave town just yet," Clint said. "We know well enough they can't carry everything they were after in saddlebags."

"They'll be after the gold as well," Allan said. "Let's get to it before they do."

"Unless they already beat us to it," Clint pointed out.

"Then let's make sure of it."

When everyone started making their way up the street, George let out a tired sigh.

THIRTY-SEVEN

The two men in the long coats were on Allan's payroll. Henry was the name of the man with the .45. Once he was closer and there wasn't so much gun smoke burning his eyes, Clint actually recognized the man with the scattergun.

"Hello, Wes," Clint said. "I was beginning to think someone had gotten to you."

"I haven't gone anywhere," Wes replied. His eyes still burned with the same intensity that Clint had seen before.

"Still watching over Felicia?"

"You're damn right I am, so you'd best keep your distance."

They'd reached the north end of Cruces Street by now, so Clint strode forward while saying, "Come on, George. Now's the time to earn all that money you've been making on this venture."

"Money?" George said nervously while glancing at the deadly men surrounding him. "I was just exploring an intriguing mystery. Once that strange map came into my possession—"

"Please," Allan said. "Spare me all the fancy words and the stage show."

"Stage show?"

"The innocent act. You're like everyone else. You saw a chance to claim a fortune in gold and you took it."

"Are you going to blame him for that?" Clint asked.

Grudgingly, Allan said, "I suppose not. Just so long as he doesn't try to pass himself off as some well-meaning explorer."

"Fine," George said.

Clint slapped his hand on George's shoulder and shoved him toward Ramon's shop. "And he can also do me a favor by no longer trying to stall. We've come this far and the only way this is going to work out properly is if we charge straight ahead without delay."

George shrugged free of Clint's grasp and stomped forward at his own pace. "I'm going!"

When they got to Ramon's front door, the entire group fanned out so they could watch the street as well as both sides of the building. There were six of them in all, counting Felicia, who carried a shotgun. Standing to one side of the door, Clint knocked.

"Ramon?" he shouted. "You in there?"

During business hours, Ramon normally kept his door open. On the rare occasions when it was closed, he hardly ever made anyone wait more than two knocks before coming to see what he could do for them. After four knocks without a response, Clint knew something was wrong.

"Landry's already been here," he said.

"Makes sense to me," Allan replied. "He'd want to come for the gold first."

"Let's check on that," Clint said before trying the door's handle. It came open so easily that Clint was certain the door had been forced open before his arrival.

"George," Clint whispered. "Stand aside. Allan, you're with me."

More than willing to follow that order, George moved away from the door so the other man could take his place.

Clint counted down four seconds using his fingers and then shoved the door open all the way. He and Allan moved in quickly and cautiously to face whatever was inside.

The small room, usually neatly arranged, was a mess. Every piece of furniture that wasn't nailed to the floor was overturned. Portions of the counter were smashed. Every tool was tossed to the floor. Ramon's scales looked like they'd been crushed beneath several stomping boots.

"Where's the safe?" Clint asked.

"Beneath the floor," George told him. "Back room."

"I'll check on it."

Clint walked behind the counter and to the narrow door that was always kept closed and, presumably, locked. Before he got close enough to reach for it, he saw it was ajar. Knowing he couldn't possibly do any more damage to the shop, he kicked open the door so it would smash against anyone trying to hide behind it. The door smacked against bare wall and rattled in its frame, revealing a modest office with half a floor.

"Whoever was here," Clint announced, "they already knew where to look." He approached the portion of the floor that had been ripped up and stared down through the gaping hole in the boards. Beneath the floor, as promised, was Ramon's safe. In fact, when Clint took a closer look, he saw there were two more safes down there to match the first.

Allan stepped into the office as well and took in the sight before him. "Damn," he gasped. "Three safes?"

"Could be more," Clint said. "There's still some floor that wasn't disturbed. Ramon had a thriving business going here."

"I'll say. Should we bother trying to open them the easy way or just start rigging up a pulley to get them out of there?"

"Right now, we keep watch over them for a while. I'm guessing the gold is still in there. If that's the case, Landry will have to come back here to get it."

Clint hadn't been speaking very loudly, but the shop was small enough for his voice to carry all the way through it and back again. "Let 'em come," Wes said. Those words were quickly followed by the metallic sounds of guns being prepared to fire.

Looking around, Clint said, "We were supposed to come here. Landry and whoever else was counting on greed to bring us here just as we were counting on it to do the same for them. The only difference between us and them is that they were here first and got a chance to prepare for when we'd do the same."

"Allan," Felicia said from the front of the shop. "You'd better come take a look at this."

Striding to the front window, Allan stood beside her and looked outside. "Aw hell," he grunted.

Clint stayed in the back office. He didn't need to see what was going on in the street. He could hear plenty. Mostly, he could hear the rumble of horses' hooves against the dry desert ground coming from all sides of the building. There was a small window over what was left of Ramon's bookshelves. Clint looked through it to see those horses taking positions in the lot behind the shop. The men in their saddles were armed with shotguns and rifles. Clint's rifles, to be exact.

"Where's the squirrelly fella?" Allan asked.

Wes was busy shoving broken pieces of furniture in front of the door. "He's gone. She let him go."

Turning his seething eyes toward her, Allan asked, "Is that true, Felicia?"

"What was I supposed to do?" she said while handing more broken pieces over to Henry, who took them to the pile Wes was building. "He wanted to get out of here and he left. Should I have shot him?"

"No, but . . ." Looking over at the men by the door, he said, "What the hell were you two doing?"

"We were looking at the men gathering outside and that fidgety little prick slipped out the door."

Allan looked outside to see a pair of horses facing George, who stood looking up at the riders. "Some partner you picked, Adams."

"Don't worry about him," Clint said. "He's just doing his part."

THIRTY-EIGHT

George had waited for his moment, and when it came, he was almost too scared to act. Once he set foot out that front door and started running toward the gathering horses, he couldn't help but feel better just for being away from the others. Before he could dwell on the shame that followed, he was looking up at Cal Landry and a gunman with the cold, dead eyes of a snake.

"Hold your fire," Landry said.

At first, George thought Landry was speaking to him. Then he noticed the riders on the street all had rifles to their shoulders and were aiming at him. They obeyed the command Landry had given them, but were itching for an excuse to pull their triggers.

Landry's eyes weren't cold, and they were far from dead. They had the glint of a knife blade that had been chipped on a rock. George couldn't stare into them for long before looking away.

"So did you come to offer something or are you just too yellow to stand in there with your partners and take your medicine?" Landry asked.

"Oh, I've got something to offer," George said. "That's for certain."

"Good. Because if you think you're getting a pardon because you're out here instead of in there, you're dumber than you look."

When he hooked his thumbs over his belt, George was trying to look like he was at ease. The others around him didn't appreciate how close his hand was to his holster, and when he moved them up, they all drew tight as bowstrings. George eased his hands out to the sides and then up so they were nowhere near his guns.

Landry gave one of his men a nod. "How about you take them weapons away from him before he gets himself killed?"

The man climbed down from his saddle and started plucking the guns from George's holsters.

"Those men inside plan to kill you," George said. "All of you."

Smirking, Landry said, "Excuse me if I'm not shaking in my boots. They ain't exactly in a position to threaten anyone."

"One of them is Clint Adams. Do you know who that is?"

"I heard a few things about him."

"Then you should know he can gun half of you down without a thought," George said. "And the other men in there with him can gun down the rest."

"Is that what you came out here for?"

"I came out here to cut my losses," George said earnestly. "And to tell you that if you try to storm that shop in the hopes of cleaning out your competition, you won't leave this town alive. None of you."

Even though the gunman closest to George was carrying all three of the captured pistols along with one of his own, he seemed a bit rattled by that. He and the other men looked to Landry for what was coming next.

"All right. Consider us warned." Landry drew his pistol, thumbed back the hammer, and pointed it squarely at George's face. "Now give me a reason not to cut one of my losses right now."

"Because you can't get into Ramon's safes," George said in a rush. "And you sure as hell can't just pick them up and ride away with them."

"We're working on getting the combinations from the blowhard who runs that shop."

"He won't tell you."

"I can be awfully persuasive," Landry said with a cruel smile.

"It'll still take time. Think you can get the job done before *El General* gets here?"

"What do you know about that?"

"I don't know all the specifics," George said. "But I'm sure you'd look a whole lot better to the old man if you had his gold stacked up nice and pretty for him when he arrived."

Landry shrugged and looked around at his men that were nearby. "You saying you know the combinations?" he asked.

"I can get them easier than you could. I'm a paying customer. Ramon trusts me. But more importantly, I can make sure you get that map back."

Landry held out one hand, palm up. "Then give it over."

"Adams took it," George said. "For safekeeping. And if you men storm that place, the map will be put to a match. I just want this to be over. Those men in there," he said while pointing to the store, "they want things to get bloody. Allan Preston wants you men to die, and he wants to do it so the old man gets a message when he arrives. All I'm asking for is a small cut of the gold I found. Just enough for a small profit. Consider it a fee for handing over those men."

"And I'm supposed to think you had this change of heart just now?"

"Think whatever you like," George told him. "But I already dug my grave the moment I ran out here. They're watching me right now, probably deciding who gets to be the first to shoot me for turning my back on them."

"Can't say as I blame 'em," said the gunman who still carried all of George's weapons.

"I can work with you to help get this squared away," George said. "I can make you look real good for your boss."

"Shut him up and keep him out of my way," Landry said. That was all his men needed to hear for them to swarm on George and drag him away from the front of the shop. Once he'd been tied to a hitching post, George was gagged and left with one man to watch over him.

The gunman who returned to Landry's side still carried George's pistols like trophies. "You think he's got anything to say to that Jeb'll want to hear?"

"Hell if I know," Landry replied. "But we won't have to wait long to find out."

THIRTY-NINE

Clint, Allan, Felicia, and the two gunhands who'd accompanied them into Ramon's shop spent the next several hours with their backs to a wall. Every so often, they took quick glances out of the shop's windows to see that Landry and his men were still right where they'd been the last time they'd checked.

"You sure about this?" Felicia asked.

Clint nodded. "I've already told you. There's only a couple of ways for this to end and they're all in our favor."

"You could have told us your partner was gonna make a run for it," Allan said. "He wouldn't have had to sneak out like that."

"As far as he knew, any one of you might shoot him if you knew why he was going to leave us."

"Not if we knew there was a good reason."

"There's an even better reason for him to think he had to escape behind your backs," Clint explained. "He needed to be scared as hell when he met up with those gunmen outside. That way, he's just convincing enough to get the job done."

"Landry isn't stupid," Felicia said. "He'll know something isn't right."

Clint looked out the window with mounting interest. "That's fine," he said. "George was just supposed to nudge them in the right direction and spark a fire beneath them."

"Then what?"

"Then it's our job to fan the flames. Speaking of which," Clint added, "it looks like it's time to do our part. Is that Jeb riding up to join Landry and the others out there?"

Both Felicia and Allan went to the front window and peeked outside, where four riders drew their horses to a stop after joining the group of gunmen surrounding the shop. One of them was an old man with impeccably trimmed whiskers and a duster that draped over the back of his horse. The other three kept close to him and watched the shop and Landry's men with equal diligence.

"That's him," Allan said. "Those three with him are cold-blooded killers who'd murder a priest or anyone else if the old man gave the order."

After a few more seconds of talking among themselves, the old man sat tall in his saddle and spoke in a bellowing voice that rolled down the street to fill Ramon's shop. "Are you really in there, Adams?" he shouted.

Leaning close to the window so he could be heard, but not so close that he could be shot, Clint replied, "I'm here."

"If you wanted to work for me again, all you needed to do was ask!"

"I didn't want any part of this."

"Then ride away."

Clint leaned over so he could take another look through the window. Although the men in the street hadn't come any closer, they'd fanned out to form a firing line. "It's too late for that," he said. "I can't just stand by and let more people get killed."

"People get killed every day," Jebediah said. "Look around. There isn't even anyone trying to stop us here! Folks just find a spot to hide and wait for the shooting to stop. When we're done, they'll go about their lives. There's no law apart from what the strong men enforce. It's like that here as well as back home. We take care of our own business for the good of the whole. Surely you must have heard about the good I've already done."

"Even if I'm to believe half of what I've heard," Clint said, "that's too much blood spilled in the name of a crazy dream."

"Crazy dream? I'm building an empire. I'm acquiring land and running it how I see fit. That's what our country was built on!"

"From what I've seen, you've got a bunch of killers working for you. Those killers have tried to gun me down more than once over a bunch of gold. That makes you no better than any other robber."

"And you're the man who put the guns into that robber's hands!" Jebediah roared. A few silent moments passed so he could collect himself. When he spoke again, his voice was smooth and even. "It's my gold, Adams. The things in those caves are mine. Even these rifles are mine. A man can't be a robber if he's taking what already belongs to him."

"Good point," Clint replied. "So let's put an end to this right now. We can all be out of here in time for supper."

"That's a splendid idea. Where's that nephew of mine and that pretty little granddaughter?"

Clint drew a deep breath and faced the others in that shop with him. "All right. This is it. Now we'll see where Jeb's heart truly is."

"Damn it, I already told you where it is," Allan snarled.

"Don't you want to be sure?"

"Yes," Felicia said. "Clint's right. We need to be sure."

Now it was Allan's turn to fill his lungs. After a slow exhale, he looked to Clint and asked, "You're sure about this?"

"It's what I do."

"What the hell," Allan sighed. "Henry, Wes, you two don't need to go with us."

Wes shrugged. "We're as good as dead if we don't. Might as well gamble."

Before any of them could change their minds, Clint stood in front of the window with his hands held high. Allan, Felicia, and everyone else that was left inside the shop did the same.

"It's good to see you all in one place," Jebediah said with an approving nod. "It'll be even better to put an end to this troublesome business." He then raised his hand, held it high for a count of one, and dropped it in a sharp chopping motion.

Without a moment's hesitation, Landry and all of the others flanking him opened fire.

FORTY

Clint, Allan, and everyone inside Ramon's place dropped to the floor. The first barrage shattered the window and punched holes through the wall and the front door. Broken glass and wood splinters rained over all of those who hunkered down with their faces pressed against the floor. In a matter of seconds, the roar of gunfire took a different tone. Along with the shots, louder explosions rippled through the air followed by cries of pain and angry swearing. Clint lifted his head just enough to get a look through the window.

Outside, half of the men had either fallen from their saddles or dropped where they stood. The scent of burnt gunpowder mixed with the acrid scent of scorched metal. The men who were still upright looked around in confusion at what had happened to the others.

When Clint stood up to go outside through the front door, Allan was right behind him.

Two of Landry's men were splayed on the ground in a bloody mess. One was missing a good portion of his face and didn't move. The other could only twitch in pain while nursing what remained of his mangled right hand.

Although shocked by the turn of events, Jebediah's gunmen were quick to react. Clint, however, was quicker. When the old man's guards took aim with their pistols, Clint drew his Colt and fired with deadly precision. Two of the guards were knocked clean off their horses, and once Allan opened fire, the other two followed them straight to hell. A few of Landry's men rushed around from the back of Ramon's shop, only to be cut down by covering fire from Henry and Wes, who'd emerged from the broken storefront.

The remaining gunmen put up a fight until Landry himself caught a bullet in the chest and dropped into a heap. A few more shots put down the last of the gunmen who wanted to fight, leaving only one with the good sense to hold his bloody hands over his head and surrender.

Jebediah had a gun in his hand, but was too stunned to use it. He barely even noticed when Allan stepped up to him and took the pistol away. "Wh-What happened?" the old man asked. "What happened?"

The gunshots had faded but the smoke still hung in the air. Clint reached down for one of the rifles used by Landry's men and held it up for all to see. The weapon's firing mechanism was blasted apart, leaving the metal casing and trigger badly scorched. "This is what happened," he said.

Jebediah looked down at the rifle. "That's one of mine."

"No," Clint snapped. "It's one of mine. I had a friend of mine buy me some time so I could fix every last one of these to backfire."

"I don't understand."

"I believe there's a saying, Uncle Jeb," Allan said. "It's got something to do with giving a man enough rope to hang himself."

"This could have all been settled amicably," Clint told him. "Not one shot had to be fired."

"But Cal—he—he told me that you were going to burn my map," Jebediah sputtered. "He said we couldn't storm the place."

"That wasn't your only choice, Grandpa," Felicia said as she stepped out of the store. "You've hurt too many people. All in the name of money. We've got plenty of money. This madness ends here and now."

Jebediah's head drooped forward. Whether it was due to the reminder of how quickly fortunes could turn or the sight of his own kin lining up against him, he suddenly lost the last bit of fight left in him. Allan helped him down from his horse while Wes and Henry walked over to George and freed him. George's guard surrendered without a fight, then Wes took charge of him and the last wounded gunman.

"Clint!" George said as he hurried over to him. "Are you all right?"

"Yeah. I'm fine. None of these rifles made it, though."

"Wasn't that the plan?"

"Sure it was," Clint said. "They were still some mighty fine pieces. It's a shame to see them go."

"It's a shame to see all of this go. Especially after the trouble we went through to get it."

"If you're talking about the gold," Allan said, "it's yours. You earned it."

"Are you sure about that?" Clint asked.

Allan nodded. "Our family has enough money as it is, and we'll make up for what we lost when we sell off the property that was so damn important to Uncle Jeb. The Prestons will still be wealthy ranchers in Texas, which is where we belong."

Felicia nodded as she watched her grandfather being

led away by Henry. "I don't want to see another one of those damn coins again."

Slapping his hands together and rubbing them vigorously, George said, "All right then. Now we've just got to find Ramon!"

Watch for

THE COUNTERFEIT GUNSMITH

393rd novel in the exciting GUNSMITH series
from Jove

Coming in September!